HIS BROKEN HEART

THE DIVIDED HEARTS SERIES
BOOK TWO

MICHELLE BOLANGER

Published by Risen Fiction Publishing

7522 Timber Valley Dr

Franklin, OH 45005

www.RisenFiction.com

ISBN 978-1-969047-08-4 (Paperback)

eISBN 978-1-969047-09-1 (eBook)

Cover Art and Interior Design by Shonda Ramsey

Printed in the United States of America First Edition 2025

10 9 8 7 6 5 4 3 2 1

20251111

AUTHORS NOTE

Dearest Reader,

Even though this story comes second in the reading order, it was the last one I wrote. It's the story I could never finish. Baden has always been the shadow character. His voice and personality is one I've struggled to connect with. He's quiet, even in my head, perhaps because his pain runs so deep. He doesn't share what's going on inside him easily, so he had to be paired with a female who won't accept anything less than his total transparency.

Dani is his opposite in every way. She's brash, outgoing, and a risk taker from the get go. But she's also fiercely loyal, whip smart, and intuitive. She knows Baden is broken and hurting, and she understands why. She's willing to give space for him to heal and grieve what he's lost, but she's going to make him admit it and face it head on.

The chase is on!

A car door slammed at the back of the house, and Dani wiped her hands on the towel as masculine laughter floated in the screen door. Glancing at the table, she stuck her tongue out at the lumpy, sideways leaning cake. Cooking was far from her best skill, but she couldn't let her youngest brother's sixteenth birthday go without cake.

The worn wood door creaked open then cracked against the frame as her closest brothers, Zane, two years older than her and Zachary, twelve years younger, came inside. The breeze swept their familiar sandalwood and mint scents toward her.

A subtle hint of floral sweetness, probably from the lilacs their mother planted along the porch, followed them inside. Their matching black hair and sharply angled features marked them as Parish boys, but the similarities ended there.

Zach raked his unkept locks away from his face and kicked his orange and white high-tops off, sending them in the general direction of the mat beside the back door. Slim fit jeans hung loose around his hips, making him look thinner than he actually was. The sixteen-year-old's style consisted of layered t-shirts, hoodies, and button-ups over expensively ripped jeans and thermal tights. The haphazard look suited his devil-may-care personality, and his youthful, minty-cocoa scent fit him perfectly.

Zane, on the other hand, had a more unique take on clothing. Steady, honest, and deeply caring, his sandalwood and myrrh scent hinted that there was more to him than what you could see, and his clothing choices dared you to look. A dark, pleated skirt hit him about mid-thigh, and she frowned at the green and gold mandala on the t-shirt under his black sport coat. *Her* t-shirt, actually. She and Zane regularly raided each other's closets, and while she was pretty good with fashion, it was hard not to envy his sense of style, especially when his makeup was as on point as his outfits.

A warm sense of contentment settled over her as the boys crossed into the hall. The three of them were extremely close. No surprise really. She and Zane raised the youngest Parish after their parents died. Though their next oldest brother, Victor, and his wife, Alana, had also lived in the house to keep things legal when at fourteen and twelve, Dani and Zane took over running the Parish household, better known as the homestead. A moniker their parents had given the house and surrounding acreage.

Built by their grandfather not long after her mother was born, the sprawling farm house was a little over two hundred years old. Her mom inherited it as a gift when she and her father announced they were pregnant with Dani's oldest brother, Able. By the time Zane was born, twenty years and fourteen boys later, the house had more additions than it had original rooms. When Dani was born, the first girl among fifteen older brothers, The Homestead had become more than simply a family home. It was a sanctuary where they could congregate as a group without having to explain to anyone why they were all boys.

Now, with only the three of them most of the time, the house felt more like a museum than a home. But none of them could bear the thought of selling. So, she, Zane, and Zachary stayed, though it had grown increasingly difficult for Zane to live this far from his studio.

And if the data in the email on Dani's computer was true, she would likely be traveling to Ireland soon. The team of hackers she'd been organizing were close to breaking into the rogue Vampir's systems, but their inside help had gone silent. Her contact indicated the mole was close to being discovered, and they were planning to get them to a safer location. That same contact seemed to think their progress would be accelerated if the two of them worked together in person, and that lead to the invite to Ireland.

Her brothers bantered in the dining room, and their easy laughter made her eyes sting with gratitude. She dreaded the day Zane would have to move, and smiled as he bent to straighten Zach's shoes, then he slipped off his light grey Toms and tucked them under the hall tree. He would deny it, but Zane was the glue that kept the three of them together.

All sixteen of her brothers were successful and, with the exception of Zane and Zach, they had married amazing women, but not one of her brothers had a Vampir mate. As huge as her family was, when she bonded - if she bonded - the change of her last name meant there would be no more Parish's to continue their bloodline. Her jaw tightened. They would be one more family name of their people gone extinct. It was why she hadn't agreed to go. Keeping her family together as long as possible was more important, and leaving Zachary wasn't something she was willing to do.

She shook those thoughts off as Zach chattered excitedly.

"Does this mean I can drive your Camaro?" Zach walked backward into the kitchen and, divesting himself of his backpack, he started to drop it in the middle of the floor but caught himself when Zane raised a brow.

Dani lurched forward when he set it blindly on the table, nearly on top of the cake. *Not that it would have made much difference.* She scowled as the cake toppled another inch sideways at the impact. She glowered at it, then met Zane's bemused eyes.

"You can drive my car anytime," Zane replied. Dani opened her mouth to protest, but he winked at her and continued. "As soon as you get a passing grade in English."

She covered her choked laugh with a cough. Zach was incredibly smart, but reading and spelling had always been a struggle for him.

"Deal!" Unfazed, Zach fist pumped and turned to Dani with a wide grin. "I passed the driver's test on the first try!"

"Of course you did." She held out her hand. "Let's see it."

He reached into his back pocket and proudly removed the brand-new driver's license from his wallet.

As she took it from him, the air bled from her lungs. No DMV photo was ever flattering, but for the first time ever, she noticed the shadow of a beard and the sharp angles of Zach's grown-up cheeks and brows. The card in her hand blurred. He wasn't a little kid anymore.

A long arm snaked across her shoulders, and she looked up expecting Zane, but Zach grinned down at her. When did he get so tall?

His smile faded, and his cheerfully minty scent shifted with a biting edge of worry. "Is something wrong?"

"No." She dropped her gaze back to the card and blinked furiously, refusing to let either of them see her wipe away tears. "I'm just proud of you."

His arm tightened and the whisper of sweetness from the lilacs returned.

"Then why are you crying?" he asked.

Feeling Zane watching them intently, she pursed her lips and shook her head. Zach folded her against his chest as his words set the tears loose.

"I wish Mom and Dad were here, too."

She sucked in a ragged breath of his scent then held on fiercely as reality crashed in.

How had she missed it?

Joy and disbelief chased each other through her chest.

The floral scent wasn't from her mother's lilacs. It couldn't be.

Not only were the bushes at the front of the house, six rooms away, but they'd dropped their blooms months ago.

She pressed her cheek to his chest and inhaled deeply. Zach's natural double layer of mint and chocolate scent did have the telltale third layer.

Not the end after all.

"Dad would be proud of the man - the male - you're becoming."

Zach pulled back to look her in the eyes. "They would both be proud of you, Nini." He swiped a finger into the icing of the cake and grinned. "But your baking could really use some work."

Zane watched them from the doorway. "Go on." He tossed Zach the keys and nodded toward the driveway. "Go celebrate with your friends."

"Thank you!" Zach caught the keys and shoved his wallet back into his pocket. "I'll be home by nine. I promise!"

He bolted out the door before Dani could say another word. "Does he know where he's going? Where *is* he going?" She whirled on Zane. "You can't just send him out without knowing those things!"

"He'll be fine." Zane moved his brothers backpack to a chair and picked up one of the forks she'd laid out. "All of us survived. He will too."

She hurried to the front window, twitching aside the curtains to watch her baby brother drive away from the house.

Zane's reflection joined hers in the glass. "He's a good kid. You raised him well. Mom would be proud of you."

"It took both of us." She dropped the curtain and crossed her arms. What she'd scented from Zach changed things. "They want me to join up with the team in Ireland."

Zane sat in Dad's old wingback chair, crossing his legs. "I thought you said you weren't going."

"That's what I told them." She glanced toward the window. "Because I didn't want to be away from Zach." Her eyes stung. "It's hard enough knowing I'll live longer than all of you. I have plenty of time to find my mate. Zach doesn't."

He straightened, his perfectly manicured brow creasing. "Are you saying he has the marker?"

She smiled slightly, excited and terrified all at once. "I scented it just now. His mate is out there somewhere, but the Vampir are too scattered." She tightened her arms around herself. "What if he never gets the chance to meet her?"

Zane leaned forward, toying with a seam in his skirt. "So, you're going?"

She turned pleading eyes on him. "For his sake, I have to. She's out there. She has to be." She didn't allow herself to hope for her own mate, but if the team could get the other clans to trust them enough to re-unite…

"He's out there," Zane said softly, then firmly. "Go. I don't have any shows for the next several months, and the rest of us will be here with Zach."

"Thank you." She sighed. "There's always hope, right?"

"Always." He stood. "Unless it involves your cake."

She followed his gaze to where the cake had slid completely from the cake stand to the table, where it lay in a broken heap of icing and crumbled chocolate.

TWO

BADEN

The college crowd chanted and clapped in anticipation of Koen Lockton's final song. Baden's chest vibrated with the thrum of the bass and kick of the drum through the stack of speakers at the edge of the stage. Every beat counted down the seconds until he would be forced to abandon Leis to a male she barely knew.

He held her in front of him with her back resting against his chest as she stared up at the male onstage with wonder. He reflexively tightened his arms around her waist. Nothing in him wanted to let her go, but staying with him would likely mean death for both of them.

Her hands rested lightly on his forearms as he scanned the crowd for any sign of her family. To their left, he spotted Andrew pushing through the crowd toward them. Baden locked eyes with him, and ignoring the pain behind his ribs, he leaned close and practically shouted in her ear to be heard over the music and voices around them.

"Remember when I said I wouldn't have time to say goodbye?" he asked.

Andrew cupped his hands to his mouth, but his words were lost in the noise. Baden shook his head as Leis turned in his arms until they were chest to chest.

Her wide green eyes looked up at him in confusion and fear, making the words stick in his throat, but he couldn't put it off any longer. She belonged with Koen, not him. He pushed every bit of courage into his scent that he could and hoped it would be enough to get her through the next few hours until Koen could explain it all to her.

"You need to run when I tell you to run, okay?" He touched her cheek and let the wrongness of being this close to her fully register. He pulled her flush against him and suppressed the painful shudder as ice seemed to coat his skin everywhere they touched. "Get backstage and go with Lockton. He'll be waiting for you." The forced contact made his stomach churn.

"Lockton? You mean Koen?" Leis's face wrinkled in pain, and she flattened her palms on his chest and pushed, but he resisted and held tighter when she tried to squirm free. "Aren't you going with me?"

He didn't look up when Andrew called out from a few steps away.

"I don't have time to explain." This was not how he'd wanted to let her go, but there was no more time. He met her terrified gaze and hated himself, but this was the only way. "You are going to run backstage, and he is going to get you away from here." Disgust rippled through him as he groped at her as inappropriately as he dared. "I love you, Leis," he said and slammed his mouth down on hers.

She went rigid in his arms, then shoved him away before landing a slap to his cheek hard enough to whip head to the side. "Stop it!"

He gritted his teeth to keep from lashing back at her.

"Nice. Now run!" He pointed toward the side of the stage and made eye contact with Andrew who stood frozen and wide eyed. Leis reached out to touch his stinging cheek, but he batted her hand away. "Run!" he commanded and pushed every ounce of courage he could into his scent. The fear in her eyes hardened into determination the second before she turned and did what he said.

Wasting a few precious seconds of his own escape time, he watched until she disappeared around the edge of the stage and then wove his way deeper into the crowd that was chanting Koen's name. He bit the inside of his cheek in an effort to keep himself focused on his next move away from the only family he had left.

"Dietrich, wait!" Andrew's voice cut through the screaming crowd as Koen's final song ended.

Baden didn't look back as he pushed blindly through the people. He cursed and dodged between elbows and open containers of beer, barely managing not to take a swing at someone blocking his path. Andrew called out again, closer. Baden lowered his head, trying to blend in and get the other male lost in the tangle of people.

He pushed through the outer fringe of the crowd and exhaled in relief until a hand clamped around his right arm. He took an instinctive step back and raised his free elbow to deliver a blow, but instead, he landed on his back with a grunt of surprise and pain.

Unbridled rage whipped through him and looked up to find Andrew leaning over him.

"Why didn't you listen to me?" He yanked Baden to his feet and gave him a shove toward the exit. "I'm here to help you."

Shock made Baden stumble, but he quickly recovered and planted his feet. If he stalled, it would give Leis and Koen more time. The thought of them together made his temples throb, but he shoved image away and squared up with Andrew.

"Help me how? You weren't supposed to be here." Baden gestured behind him.

"None of us were!" Andrew threw up his hands. "I came to help distract Dad and Mom. For now, I sent them in the opposite direction." Andrew jutted his chin toward a distant parking lot across the field. "We need to get you out of here before they figure out I lied."

He made to step around him, and Baden's heart charged against his ribs as he braced a hand on the other man's chest.

"Why should I believe you?"

"I've been helping you hide for years, and you're asking me this now? Besides, you're not the only one who cares about my sister." Andrew leaned in, and Baden couldn't tell if it was regret or guilt that flashed in his eyes. "I want her out of that house as much as you do."

"This wasn't part of the plan."

He exhaled in a puff and stalked toward the main gate. "The plan went in the trash the moment Res sent Dad and Mom out here." Andrew shot a glare over his shoulder as he broke into a jog. "Move, Dietrich. Trust me or don't, but neither of us can stay here."

The sound system crackled as the announcer dismissed the crowd, which would send the horde of people behind him for the exit. He needed to stay ahead of them if he had any hope of escaping. Could he risk following Andrew? It appeared he didn't have any choice, but how much of the plan was changed? His shoes skidded in the loose gravel as he banked through the open gate and caught up to Andrew.

"The car is two blocks away on Maple Avenue, right?" Andrew spared him a glance and kept jogging.

"That's what I was told." Baden fell into step beside him.

"Then we are going to Third. I left a bike there." He pulled a set of keys from his pocket and tossed them.

Baden caught and fisted them. "How did you do that?"

"Ellen." He grinned as they increased their pace. "I asked if she could get one. I even got you a helmet. It will foil the cameras."

They had to hurry. He led the way down an alley, cutting through toward Third Street a block and a half away. In less than five minutes the area would be gridlocked. Their steps fell into a familiar rhythm on the sidewalk, and he closed his eyes for a second.

How many miles had he jogged side by side with Andrew? They were best friends with years of memories between the two of them. They'd laughed and planned out their life and shared stories about family. Andrew had kept his secrets, and trusting him should be easy, but the thought made his gut tighten. Trusting someone they thought was a friend got his parents killed.

He scanned the buildings and altered his cadence as they slowed to cross a street. It was a dirty trick, but one they'd pulled on each other during cross country races. Andrew instinctively adjusted his stride, then stumbled when they rounded a corner. Baden seized the opportunity and shoved Andrew toward the raised stoop of a doorway, but in one quick move, he reversed and planted Baden's cheek against the bricks.

"What is wrong with you?" he snapped.

Baden squirmed in his grip. "Why are you here?"

"You want to know why I'm here?" Andrew yanked him around and held him against the wall with an arm across his throat. Baden was too stunned to react when Andrew snarled in his face. "You know what your grandmother is trying to do. Why *wouldn't* I be here?" He let go and stepped back. "I met with Ellen two days before your grandmother sent us out here to bring you and Leis back to Arizona." His hand shook as it ran through his hair. "I promised her I would get you on your way."

Baden tugged his shirt straight and shrugged the pain out of his shoulder. "And what are you going to do once I'm gone?"

"I'll tell them I chased you, but you got into a car before I could catch you." He turned back up the sidewalk. "The bike is up here."

Traffic was non-existent when they approached the low slung cruiser. It was larger and louder than the one he had stashed, but it fired up smoothly as Andrew handed him the helmet.

"Get going." He tapped one of the saddle bags. "All the documents you'll need are here. Where is your phone?"

Baden tapped his front pocket. "I have it."

"Give it to me." He held out his hand. "If it's tracked, we should put it in the car you were supposed to take."

Reluctantly, Baden handed it to him. "Is there another in the bag?"

Andrew shook his head. "I don't know. But you should go dark for a while. Get to wherever you're going and get a new one there."

His chest tightened but he nodded. Andrew was right. He couldn't carry anything that would be trackable, but it felt like cutting off a limb. He pulled the helmet over his head and lowered the smoke-colored shield.

Andrew tucked the phone into his back pocket and patted him on the back. "Get going. I've got your back, Dietrich."

With a last glance toward the college grounds, Baden revved the engine, then pulled away from the curb.

CHAPTER
THREE

DANI

Dani had to admit the Dublin airport smelled like every American airport she'd been in and gave her the same headache. Woven among the normal scents of strong coffee, greasy food, and sugary pastries, the emotions of the people flooded her senses. Excitement and frustration mingled as she passed the boarding gate of a plane that had just been delayed, but she tuned them all out as best she could. She couldn't afford to get distracted.

Dragging her hastily packed carry-on behind her, she navigated between the crowds and found the baggage area where her escort would be waiting. From the escalator, she scanned the area and spotted him standing with a group of men near the luggage claim with her plane's number on it.

Connell Lynch was instantly recognizable. Tall with shaggy blond hair and broad shoulders, he'd visited the States a few years ago to help set up the network she'd flown to Dublin to rebuild. Since she knew and trusted him, he had been assigned as her bodyguard for the duration of her trip to Ireland.

He spotted her almost immediately and lifted his chin in acknowledgment as he nudged the man beside him. Four more heads turned her way, and she fought the urge to cringe. They looked like a flock of birds as they moved as a group in her direction. Other than Connell's height and the way he seemed to be more aware of their surroundings than the others, not one of them looked like the security team Ellen promised.

She lost sight of them as she reached the bottom of the escalator and her nostrils flared as a pair of men headed straight for her. Their focus didn't waver from her, and she tightened her grip on the rolling case, prepared to shove it into their shins until a stray breeze swept their scents to her. Humans.

They split, one to her right and the other to her left. A woman behind her shrieked in recognition. Dani kept moving but risked a glance over her shoulder in time to see one of the men sweep her in his arms. A smile tugged at the corner of her mouth as he set her down and swept a hand over her pregnant belly in wonder. As he bent to kiss her, Dani slammed to a stop against a wall of muscle.

Her skin vibrated with the wrongness of the male's touch, and she sucked in a breath. Only the fact that she recognized his cinnamon scent saved Connell from getting a knee in a very uncomfortable place. He grinned down at her, but his thick Irish lilt had an edge.

"Welcome to Dublin, Miss Jordan." He opened his arms mockingly. "Would you prefer a greeting like that one?"

The rest of the men closed around her, and she couldn't resist a hopeful indrawn breath as all five of them waited for her reaction to Connell's offer. Though their scents were each distinct, they blended into a heady mix of earth, musk, and masculine sweetness. But none of them belonged to her mate. She suppressed the ache of disappointment from her echo and shot Connell a wicked smirk.

"Touch my belly, and I'll break your fingers," she said, relieved when her saucy tone elicited snorts of relief from the other men.

"Sounds like my kin'a girl." A dark-haired man shouldered his way in front of Connell. "Finley Porter." He held out a hand, but she just stared until he dropped it. "So, that's a no then?"

Disappointment swirled in the air around her as she exhaled and pushed past them, heading for the exit. She couldn't blame them for hoping and also couldn't deny the same hope had risen in her, but none of them were her intended, and a second breath confirmed none of them had the third genetic scent marker. There would be time to tell them individually, but there was no point making them wonder about her.

"It's definitely a no. To all of you." She let a little disappointment bleed into her echo. "That would have been too easy, wouldn't it?"

A large part of her resonated with the men's eagerness. Not knowing where her intended might be or if he even existed weighed heavy with each year that passed. Leaving the States before the Gathering in Arizona meant her chance to mingle with a diverse crowd of their people would be delayed another year.

She blew out a breath. Finding her intended had to take a back seat to breaking into the compound's network.

If it hadn't been for Ellen Tate's desperate request for help, she would have ignored her brothers' warnings and risked going to the compound herself. But, the entire network of hackers they had built was in jeopardy, and she was one of two people who possessed the skill to build a new one strong enough to replace it. She had communicated with Baden, the other engineer, months ago, and the things he'd told her about his life made her chest ache for all of them under Res' control. Hopefully, he wouldn't be caught before he was scheduled to arrive a day or so after her. Even this team didn't know exactly when his flight would arrive.

Finley fell in step beside her. If he was disappointed to learn she wasn't intended for any of them, it vanished quickly, replaced by the same intense protectiveness that flowed from Connell.

Another of the men fell in step beside her. "Simple as that, eh?"

Dani jerked her head toward him. "You're human."

"Aye. Half actually." He ticked his head back to where Connell trailed the group. "I'm with Conn."

Finley took the bag from her as the glass doors slid open. "We're in the car park to the left." He gestured past a low parking garage and nudged the man in the shoulder. "I think William here was genuinely worried."

"Lay off him, Fin." Connell snapped, and she immediately understood the reservation she'd picked up from the blond, sharp eyed Irishman years ago.

At the time, she wrote it off. Most people found her huge, all male family intimidating, but staying in a house with ten men and one woman had probably been even more uncomfortable for Connell.

She looped her arm through William's. "He's all yours."

"That he is," William patted her hand. "Though I'd be lying if I didn't admit to holding my breath when one of you ladies come around."

She looked up and couldn't resist answering the question in his worried, gray-green eyes. "Don't. It's not possible."

She looked away and closed her eyes as Connell's relief deepened the sweetness of his scent.

"Thank you, Lass." William's hand tightened on hers then dropped.

The rest of them fell silent at the exchange, and a sad sense of relief rode the wind in the mix of sandalwood, peppermint, and tobacco as the air swirled around them. She was unsurprised to note a smoky hint of suppressed anger from one of them, but their faces revealed nothing, and all of their emotions were too high to figure out who it might be. A glance at each of them as they waited for Connell to unlock the van gave her a moment to sort through which scent belonged to who. The cinnamon and tobacco belonged to Connell and Finley, and a quick mental note assigned the peppermint, ginger, and mahogany to the other three whose names she hadn't learned yet.

Lingering tension made her nerves prickle, and her hand sang with pain when Finley helped her navigate into the front seat. The door closed on the new male scents, and though living with all her brothers taught her to adjust quickly to multiple males in close quarters, her sinuses hadn't caught up yet, and they throbbed in protest. She rolled the window down with an exaggerated groan.

"This is why I ride a motorcycle," she said as Connell maneuvered the van out of the lot with practiced ease.

"Why is that?" Finley, seated directly behind her, asked.

"Clean air!" She waved a hand at the van. "Mom drove six of us to school every morning." She pulled her hair over her shoulder and braided it. "I started riding my bike because it was the only way I could get to school without a headache." Several of them snorted, and she swiveled in her seat to look at them. "Please tell me I can get a decent motorcycle here."

The confined space made it even more difficult to pick individual motives from their scents, but as she briefly met each of their gazes, the overwhelming sense of unity between them was apparent. The redheaded younger boy in the back avoided looking directly at her, but he spoke up.

"My father owns a motorbike shop." His cheeks flushed, and he looked at her sideways. His sweet peppermint scent and boyish smile reminded her of Zachary. "He always has a spare."

"What's your name?" she asked.

"Ruadhrí Walsh, but everyone calls me Pep."

She narrowed her eyes playfully. "As in Peppermint?"

He lifted a shoulder. "Yeah. My sister tagged me with it, and it stuck."

"I like her already," Dani said and started to turn.

"She left the clan to go searching for her mate." The cold in Pep's voice matched the snap of snow in his scent, and she shivered at his next words. "We haven't seen or heard from her in two years."

Dani swept her eyes over the rest of them and fought back a gag as their combined pain and anger lashed at her senses. She swallowed through the tightness of her throat and faced forward.

"That's why I'm here, Pep," she said, then added with a confidence she didn't feel, "We'll be a united people again soon."

FOUR

BADEN

"The crew and I would like to welcome all of you aboard flight 654 to New York, LaGuardia." The pilot's voice barely registered as Baden slid into his row.

He settled the nearly empty brief case on his lap. The only thing inside were his travel documents. All fake, all meant to do one thing. Make him as invisible as he felt.

The seat next to him remained empty and he breathed a sigh of relief. At least he would be able to think without having to worry about a talkative seat mate. But the vacant seat seemed to mock him, reminding him once again that even on the flight, he was alone, separated from everyone.

He twisted the air vent open, hoping to alleviate the stifling air inside the plane, but closed it again when the cold breeze touched the moisture on his cheeks. Angrily, he swiped at the tears and stared out the window as the plane backed away from the terminal. He rested his temple against the wall and closed his stinging eyes. The betrayal of his control made him feel weak and small.

Crying changes nothing.

He gritted his teeth and tried to listen to the pre-flight speech in a desperate attempt to keep himself from focusing on what he'd just lost.

Everything. I've lost everything.

His family, his future, every dream and plan he'd ever had turned out to be a lie. Leis's future no longer included him. No one's did. Without his phone, laptop, or tablet, he couldn't even help the network anymore.

No one needed him. In fact, he was a liability, sent out of the country and cut off from the Clan so his presence wouldn't jeopardize the safety of everyone else.

He clenched a fist and stifled the urge to punch the seat in front of him. Unable to hold them back, he gritted his teeth against the tears streaming down his face.

Nothing. He could do nothing but run away and hide like a coward.

When the interior lights dimmed he rested his head on the seat back, fighting to regain control. He was stronger than this, and wallowing didn't change anything. In moments, the wheels were off the ground, and Baden closed his eyes.

The real pain came with the understanding he had to hope his hunch about Leis's connection to Koen was correct. Meeting the other male shouldn't have been a shock. It's why he'd worked so hard with Ellen to get them to Ohio in the first place. But somewhere deep inside, he'd wanted to be wrong.

There had never been a moment in his life when he hadn't expected to be bound to Leis. Then, every time she mentioned Koen, he heard the beginnings of her connection to him. Leaving her with the other male gutted him. He hadn't understood that phrase until now, but it perfectly described the agonizing emptiness in his stomach, though there were no words to explain the bloody mess of his heart.

Exhaustion settled over him, and he dozed off, waking when the crew wheeled a snack cart down the aisle.

"Would you like anything?" the flight attendant asked. Her

chocolate brown hair was pulled into a low chignon at the nape of her slender neck, and her quiet green eyes reminded him of Leis.

"Just coffee, please." He took the cup and cellophane packet containing the condiments. "Thank you."

With a soft smile she patted the empty seat next to him in dismissal then moved on to the next passenger.

The coffee was strong and hot. He tore open the paper packet of creamer and his mind drifted back through the letter he gave Koen for Leis. Absently stirring the creamer into his cup, the words he'd written scrolled through his head.

...I'VE KNOWN from the moment you mentioned his name Koen was one of the Clan, and he recognized you instantly. I don't know what that must have been like for him, but I hope he not only recognized what you are, but also the amazing woman you've become.

I've been told when you meet your intended mate it is unmistakable. If the attraction between you and Koen is as strong as I think it is, the likelihood is almost certain you are intended for one another...Koen will be the catalyst...you need to trust what you and Koen have. Refuse to let anyone come between you.

You will always be my best friend, and not knowing if I will ever see you again is hard. Knowing for certain that the next time I do, you'll be bonded to him, is both the happiest and saddest moment of my life.

HE TOOK a large swallow of the coffee and blamed the scalding liquid for the tears that sprang back to his eyes.

I LOVE YOU, Leisel, but you are not mine and I am not yours...please don't fight it. Let him claim you.

There was so much more he'd wanted to tell her, but it would have to wait until he could see her again.

If I see her again.

He pressed his thumb and forefinger against his eyes. Not only was he forced to leave Leis behind, but he was running for his life because the rest of his relatives likely wanted him dead. There was no way they would simply allow him to leave the Clan knowing what he knew.

A palm landed on his shoulder, and he slowly dropped the hand from his face as a familiar voice sent chills down his spine.

"Leaving is always hard." Though her tone was exactly the same as his grandmother's, this woman's echo washed all the tension from him, leaving him almost dazed.

He watched her set his briefcase on the floor before he dared look at her face. Grey hair fell in soft waves around her shoulders, and her golden eyes studied him. For a moment, his heart seized in his chest.

"Who are you?" he breathed.

She laughed softly. "Technically, I'm your aunt." She touched his shoulder again, and he blew out a shaky breath. The pride in her voice straightened his spine. "I've been watching out for you from the day you came to Ohio. I'm sorry I couldn't introduce myself sooner."

"You were at the dinner." He scanned her face and frowned. "I thought it was just a coincidence how much you looked like her. But…How did you disguise your voice?"

"When you live as long as I have, you learn a few tricks." She winked at him, then sobered. "You honestly thought we would send you out of the country alone?"

"I didn't know what to think." He let his gaze wander over the seats in front of them, then swallowed. "Is Leis safe?" he asked quietly.

She settled back in the seat, and pain edged her echo. "Neither she nor Koen have been caught. We'll know more when Emerick gets to Indiana tomorrow evening. Hopefully, they will both be with him."

"Why not call him tonight? Find out what he knows?"

"No." The pain in her voice spiked, and she held up a hand, making him wait a breath before she explained. "The entire network is ordered to go dark for the next 36 hours. By that time, everyone will be in place, and you'll be out of reach."

"But what about Leis?" Why couldn't she make a simple undetected phone call? The network wasn't that far compromised. He gripped the arms of the seat and deliberately kept his tone low. "How can you be sure she's safe? Lockton doesn't know what my grandmother is capable of! One mistake and he'll —"

"Baden." The sharp cut of her echo sliced though him, and she lowered her chin. "I need you to listen to me."

Silence rang in his head as she held his gaze and exhaled slowly. He breathed out with her and released his grip on the seat arms. When he blinked as if waking from sleep, her wry smile made him frown as the sound of people talking and the thrum of the engines pressed back into his awareness.

"Leis will be fine," she said gently. "It's you I'm most concerned about." She tilted her head. Her gaze flicked between his eyes.

He flexed his fingers, still slightly disoriented. "I'm frustrated, but fine." He rubbed a hand across his mouth. "I hate that I'm stuck on this plane. I feel useless."

"Giving up control isn't easy," she said. "You want to help Leis, to protect her like you always have, and right now you can't. That is why you feel useless." Amusement and camaraderie filled her tone as she handed him a digital notebook.

"What's this?"

"All the information you need about the parallel network. Jordan Parish and the rest of your team will coordinate with you once we arrive in Dublin." She tapped the cover. "I don't understand any of it, but they have been running this system side-by-side with the current network in anticipation of my sister breaking into the first."

He opened the cover and immediately recognized the coding.

"This is Jordan's work," he said and thumbed through a few more pages. Equations and formulas covered the screen like stanzas of music. On the left side were the formulas he'd spent years picking from his grandmother's network, altered, and then used to hide his communication with Jordan and the others. On the right was the updated version, and he immediately saw where he'd gone wrong. "Whoever this hacker is, he's much better than me." He closed the book.

"They might be better, but only because there are nine of them." She leaned forward until he met her eyes. Her warm hand covered his. "They took what you created and used it as a template to build this. I already told you I don't understand any of it, but I do know none of this would have been possible without you. The team that put this together needs your guidance before any of it can be used. They need to know what you know."

His chest tightened.

"They have been working together for a long time, and they're a tight group." She patted his hand. "But I have a feeling you'll fit right in."

"What do you know about him?" Connell asked.

Dani chewed her lip. The file containing all the pertinent information about Baden Dietrich lay scattered across the conference table between them. It was her first real look at the face behind the screen. This was the Vampir inside Res' compound she had been communicating with for almost a year.

"As much as you do, I suppose." She picked up a page with his photo on it. The male staring up at her had serious, almost haunted brown eyes and rich chestnut hair trimmed neatly above his collar. "He's Res' grandson, or great-great-grandson, and Ellen's great-great nephew." That meant he came from a wealthy family, and it showed. Handsome in a polished, academic kind of way, Baden didn't look like the kind to betray his family. She handed the picture to Connell who grunted in agreement. "We wouldn't have been able to break her coding without him."

"Do you think we can trust him?" Connell asked.

"Ellen vouched for him, and he seems genuinely determined to get his family away from Res." During several late-night chats while working to dismantle some piece of Res' security, she'd wished she could see his face, but he'd insisted the risk was too high for images. He'd been able to intuitively weave her coding into his, allowing her network to slip through the restrictions on Res' cell network. That particular opening allowed them to track Res and crack some of the restrictions that kept those under her control blinded when online.

She sorted through a stack of data entries, pulling the file on his whereabouts and flipping it open. Surprisingly, the male hadn't lived with his grandmother and rarely went anywhere other than school or local restaurants. Most of his time was spent at the home of his assigned mate, Leisel Gottschalk, and her family.

The idea of an assigned mate made no sense. How had Res convinced her followers to go along with it? Touching a male who wasn't compatible made Dani's skin itchy, sometimes to the point of pain if the connection lasted long enough. She glanced at Conn, then exhaled and leaned into her hands. "He made it clear he's willing to do whatever it takes to stop Res from forcing anymore bondings."

"When did he decide that?" Conn's grey eyes studied my face. "I mean, he's been in Res' inner circle for a long time." He settled back in his chair and crossed his arms. "She's trusted him with all her security. Are we sure he's not setting us up?"

She chewed her lip, considering. "I don't see what that would benefit. He could have just as easily locked us out rather than answering the knock I sent. Ellen said he's been hiding things from his grandmother for a very long time and decided to go against her."

"What changed?" Conn pointed to the file. "We've sent feelers into the system before. He could have responded years ago. Why now?"

"He found out she killed his parents," Dani said quietly, and met Connell's eyes. "And then to find out Leis is his first cousin because their dads were twins? That has to change things."

Conn didn't look convinced. "Even if all that is true, bringing her grandson here seems like a huge risk. What if he's coming here to shut us down or expose your location? The whole point of bringing you here is to keep you as far away from Res' people as possible."

She couldn't argue there was a chance they were wrong. She studied the data again. There were large chunks of time when none of his devices moved at all. It was strange because the telemetry could pinpoint him down to a few inches. No one sat that still for hours at a time.

Reportedly, he had been taking dance lessons for years without anyone knowing where he was. In reality, they had no idea where he'd been going or what else he'd kept hidden from his grandmother. It was hard to believe the Elder truly didn't know what he was doing. According to the trace, his phone, laptop, and watch never went anywhere out of the ordinary. The system should have flagged it as unusual, but if he was as good a hacker as she thought, he could have easily foiled his own system. Still, something in her gut told her he could be trusted.

"Let me meet him at the airport," Conn suggested. "I'll take him to my flat, and you can meet us there once I've cleared him."

She shook her head. "The plan is for him to travel alone to the studio. If you try to pick him up, it will spook him. We don't have any way to let him know the plan changed, and if he goes rogue it increases the risk to all of us."

"But are you sure leading him straight here is a good idea?" Conn gestured to the silent offices. "We can remotely destroy the hard drives and disable the software, but it will take months to rebuild if he's being followed."

"He has nothing trackable on him. Not even a thumb drive. He's gone completely dark." She opened her laptop and logged in. "Our last sighting of him was at the boarding gate when he got on the flight. I'll get an alert when the facial recognition picks him up after he disembarks in Dublin." She turned the screen to show him the video of Baden scanning his boarding pass then disappearing down the jet bridge and onto his flight from New York. "We already have tracking on the rental car, and a dash cam on the interior. We'll know every move he makes."

"What about Ellen? She's on that flight, too, right?" He asked.

"She's catching a connecting flight to Belfast. William will meet her and drive back here." She frowned. "We made this plan days ago. We can't go changing things now. There isn't time."

He crossed his arms. "I still think it's a bad idea to bring him straight here."

"This is the safest place for him to be." She gestured to the apartments above. "The whole building is dampened. Nothing gets in or out unless it goes through our network. If he's here, he's invisible." Conn knew this. He had installed the dampeners himself. She narrowed her gaze at him. "What aren't you telling me?"

His expression closed. "Why are you defending him?"

"I'm not." She looked away. "He's really good at what he does, and he deserves a safe place to go."

"Why here?" Conn pressed. "You could keep working with him from a distance. There's no need for you to meet him in person, is there?" His brow lifted a fraction.

Her heart gave a quick jump. He couldn't have read the message from Ellen. She sighed to cover the nervous hitch in her echo. "He's coming here because it's safer for all of us," she insisted.

"No other reason?" Conn's lips twitched. "He's a handsome male."

"You think so?" *Was he baiting her?* "William will be jealous."

He barked a laugh. "I suppose he would be. What about you?"

She made a face. "No. I doubt he's my type." But her heart continued to thump against her ribs. Hope was a frightening thing, and there was so much more at stake than her desire for a mate, even if Ellen seemed to believe it was possible.

I'll be honest with you, Jordan. Ellen had written before she'd boarded the flight to take her seat behind Baden. *After all that's happened, he's complicated and lost. But something tells me you might be just what his broken heart needs.*

She chewed her lip again, staring at the paperwork without really seeing it. Their lives were very different. He'd been raised with wealth and privilege. Going to private schools, wearing designer clothes and shoes, and living a sheltered life with only Leis and her brother for close friends.

Nothing about his profile felt compatible, but that didn't stop her from hoping Ellen was right.

CHAPTER

SIX

BADEN

Baden watched Ellen disembark the plane a few rows ahead of him. She'd sat beside him until the final descent into Dublin, then resumed her seat further forward. Before moving, she assured him she would catch up with him soon and would be taking another flight.

As his row moved down the aisle, he clutched the handle of the briefcase so hard his hand ached. By the time he found the rental car agency and managed to get out of the airport on the wrong side of the road, he was starving but didn't want to risk stopping to get something to eat.

He managed to follow the GPS directions without causing an accident and parked in the lot of a large stone building at the edge of a small village. Most of the route had been surrounded by rolling hills and twisty roads, and the town looked exactly like he expected Ireland to be. Narrow cobblestone lanes between stacked stone and stuccoed buildings, with tile roofs and window boxes full of trailing vines and flowers.

He stepped out of the car as the whine of an approaching sports bike drew his attention. The sound increased as the bike got closer, and several men wandered out of the building to stare up the street. He followed their line of sight. The street was wider than most in this part of town and freshly paved. On a weekday, it would probably be a main thoroughfare, but this late on a Sunday, it was nearly empty.

He stepped further onto a sidewalk made of brick pavers that looked like they had been there for centuries. Several long blocks away, the glimmer of the motorcycle's headlight pointed their way.

One of the guys shouted something with a thick accent he couldn't make out, and the rider revved the engine in response as if they had heard. With a twist of the wrist, the bike shot forward and rose onto the rear tire. As the rider approached, their helmet rose above the handlebars, and he realized they must be standing on the seat.

The group of men him cheered and waved as a newer model Ducati sailed past, and he noted with surprise the rider was undeniably female. She wore a form fitting white leather riding suit and matching helmet. The bike dropped to two tires as she grabbed the front brake and gassed it. With delicate precision, she rode the skid of the rear tire until the bike was facing back the way she'd come. A chorus of appreciative male voices made the hair at the back of his neck rise.

The rider eased the bike into a parking spot beside the building and killed the engine. She flipped the visor open, and Baden's heart stopped when her sultry Vampir echo shot through him. Not a single cell in his body was prepared for the explosion of need that rippled over his body.

"I need to work on the turn around. I nearly jumped the curb that time." Her low voice rode over his skin with the faintest hint of an accent, and the adrenaline in her tone powered the echo straight into his blood as if pure octane had been dumped into his system.

This one is mine. Sheer surprise at the realization froze the breath in his lungs, and he stared at her in shock. He wanted to run. To get far away but turning away from her was impossible. *This can't be happening.* His heart threatened to leap from his chest when, despite himself, he took a step toward her.

"You got both feet off the pegs today, Dani. Wanna celebrate the success in my office?"

Baden whipped his head around at the man's suggestive tone, and one look at his leering face made him go nearly blind with jealousy. Without thinking, he took two steps and pinned the man against the wall with an arm across his throat.

"Say that again!" Baden growled into his face.

"Ho there, Lad!" A long arm reached between them, seizing him over his shoulder and across his chest. "You might want to slow down, my good man."

The blond man leaned toward him with a taunting grin that made him tighten his fists until a blaze of white leather and long dark hair wedged between them.

"Stop it, Connell!" The female planted a hand on each of their chests, then turned wide eyes to Baden. "You?" Her nostrils flared and he watched as her eyes dilated in recognition. "You're my..." Her eyes darted to the men surrounding them, then back to his. "You're Baden."

"And he's a real prize," Connell snarled.

Tearing his gaze from the girl, Baden leaned against the arm holding him. "Apologize to her."

"For what? It wouldn't be the first time she's been in my office for a -"

The slap rang loud, and everyone froze. All eyes turned to the girl.

"Joke's over, Conn." She shook out her hand and then gave him a shove. "Go find Fin and tell him our visitor is here."

The blonde male shot Baden a glare, then turned and stalked inside.

"Go on with the rest of you." She waved at the front door. "I'll handle this."

The arm holding him loosened, and Baden shrugged it the rest of the way off. He positioned himself between Dani and the rest of the males, unable to tear his gaze away from her even as dread pooled in his stomach.

Dani didn't look at him, still glaring at the males moving away. She was taller than Leis, dark complected from sun or natural color he couldn't tell. The red crease across her forehead from the helmet she'd removed and the tendrils of hair swirling in the light breeze amplified the wildness in her eyes as she watched them, seemingly daring them to challenge her.

Some part of him reared up, wanting to shield her from their view. He half turned, realizing one of them hadn't walked away. His fists tightened as the man who'd been restraining him stepped forward with a wide grin on his face.

He lowered his voice. "Congratulations you two."

Dani's cheeks darkened. "Thank you, William. We'll be right behind you."

"Don't hurry, Love."

Baden ground his teeth, and he crossed his arms to keep from taking a swing. The sidewalk finally cleared and he exhaled. She wasn't looking at him, as she drew in a breath, shuddering on the exhale. The rush of anger and jealousy slowly bled out of him, leaving him confused.

"I'm sorry. I promise I'm not usually violent," he said roughly, raking a hand through his hair. "Other than the shock of...you, I don't have an excuse for that."

She didn't respond right away, and he took a moment to study her. The white leather suit hugged her body like a second skin, and even with the padded plates over her chest, back, shoulders, and elbows it was easy to see she was lean and fit. She kept her head down and a long, dark braid of hair slipped over her shoulder.

She reached up and he heard the faint pops of her zipper being loosened. She chuckled and the rage he'd felt only moments before was replaced by an almost hysterical amusement. Her large brown eyes were filled with laughter when they finally met his.

"I can't believe she was right."

He blinked. "Who?"

"I'm pretty sure Ellen knew this would happen." She gestured between them then shook her head, flipping the long braid over her shoulder.

"Ellen knew you're my mate?" He looked backward down the street as through the Elder would be standing behind him. Was that why she'd sent him here? Not to help the network of hackers, but so he'd meet this female? He ground his teeth. He wasn't ready. Might never be ready. And he wasn't even sure he ever wanted to be.

Instead of answering, she stalked toward her bike and plucked the glossy white helmet from the ground. "Charging Connell was a waste of time by the way. He's completely harmless. At least to women."

Baden realized his mouth was hanging open and closed it with a snap.

She spun the helmet in her hand and pointed to a scrape along the side. "Now I have to buy a new helmet. I dropped it when you and Conn decided to act like cavemen. You owe me a new one."

He moved closer, reaching for the helmet. "Tell me how Ellen knew about us, and I'll buy you anything you want," he said low. "And if she told you, why she didn't warn me as well?"

"Warn you?" Disappointment leached into her echo. Brow furrowing, she released the helmet as he took it from her. She inhaled again and eased away from him. "It was a hunch, I think. She didn't know for sure."

She still could have prepared me for the possibility. He would have avoided coming here at all costs. He glanced over his shoulder. "I'm supposed to meet a team of hackers here. Was that them?"

"Most of them." She crossed her arms. "They're good at what they do."

"They are." Turning the helmet over in his hands, he glanced at the Ducati. She rode that thing with zero fear. He tried to imagine Leis on a motorcycle but failed. She would never take those kinds of risks. He clenched his jaw hoping Koen wouldn't either. "I need to find a place to stay, and if you can tell me where I can get a bike instead of the car, and I'll buy you a new helmet."

"You ride?" She asked, genuine surprise lacing her echo.

"Not like you do, but yeah. A cruiser is more my style." He handed the helmet back to her.

She took it and huffed a laugh. "William doesn't ride his anymore. I'm sure he'll let you borrow it." Her gaze flicked to the building behind him. "I'm sorry about Conn and the rest of the guys." Regret ghosted over him. "They thought taunting you would be good for a laugh. They wanted to rattle your cage a bit."

"It's fine." He tucked his hands in his pockets. "I'm sorry I responded that way, and I'll apologize to Connell. Is he the one who goes by Jordan?"

"No." Her soft laugh and the twinkle in her eyes sent desire skating across his skin. "I'm Jordan."

He started to respond, then froze as her claim sank in. "*You're Jordan Parish?*"

She grinned. "Surprise."

CHAPTER
SEVEN

DANI

Even though Ellen had hinted he might be her mate, nothing prepared her for the heat that rushed through her body at the first whiff of Baden's scent. Connell's eyes had widened when he'd noted her reaction, and for a split second as the two males faced off, she'd closed her eyes to draw a deep breath of her mate's scent. Sweet tobacco, rosemary, and a hint of allspice blended together in a unique signature that suited the male before her perfectly.

The shock hit her first, then the aching at the roof of her mouth. Though her fangs hadn't pressed for release, the scent of his desire raced across her sinuses. Thick and rich, it was filled with subtle hints of mystery and shadows that tightened her stomach.

But, as enticing as it was, something felt off. A bitter tang hung underneath, as if the mixture had been sealed up and left in a dark, damp room. She'd thought it was anger at the taunting, but now it felt more like bitterness that had been festering for a long time. Given what she knew about his past, she shouldn't be surprised, but the longer they talked the more she got the impression he wasn't as excited to meet her as she was him. That did surprise her.

Needing to break the tension, she gestured to the entry door behind him. "There is a dance class arriving in thirty minutes. I'll give you a tour of the studio before they get here. The guys can show you the rest while I'm teaching."

He didn't move. "This can't be real."

She crossed her arms. "What? The dance studio? What did you think your cover would be?"

"Not that." The muscle in his jaw ticked, and his chestnut eyes locked on hers. "You."

"Me?" She pointed to her own chest. "Why?"

Emotions flickered across his face and his scent filled with pain and betrayal before he looked away. He raked a hand through his hair, the muscle in his jaw flexing. "Nothing."

"I'm as overwhelmed by what we are as you are." She stepped closer. "I don't expect us to..." She swallowed as his hard gaze fell to hers. "We don't need to rush anything." A wave of self-loathing crested over her so strong she reached out to lay her hand on his arm, needing to touch him. He went rigid, his scent turning pungent.

He stared at where she held his forearm then carefully peeled her hand away, dropping it as if she'd burned him. "We'll talk about us later. Tell me more about the team."

Trust won't come easily for him. Ellen had warned. *But he trusted Jordan - trusted you - he just didn't know it. You earned it without him ever meeting you. I know you can do it again.*

She exhaled, lifting her chin. Fine. He wanted to be all business; she could do that. "I'm the team lead and chief programmer. I handled any direct contact with you and the others. Connell and William handle the hardware. Finley, Pep, and myself monitor all traffic across the link between the networks."

His piercing gaze threatened to make me squirm, but I glared right back. It wasn't the first time someone was surprised a female was behind the keyboard.

"Who are the others?" He asked.

"No one you would know." She held up a hand when his eyes

narrowed. "The contact I had with them wasn't through Res' network. We're working with Vampir from all over the world. I've been the main source of contact for most of them."

"That puts a lot of people in jeopardy if everything comes to one source."

"It does," she agreed. "But a single point of failure was a risk we had to take. Giving too many people access would have been worse."

His jaw flexed again, but he nodded. "That's how my grandmother operated." He studied her. "As far as I am aware, I'm still the only one with full access to her servers, unless you were able to get in."

"Not yet. But I was hoping you'd be able to talk me through it." When he looked away she ticked her head toward the doors. "I really need to get ready for my class."

"Show me where the workstations are, and I'll get us in." He reached in front of her to grasp the door handle but didn't open it.

She looked up, inches separating their faces. Her breath caught as his free hand lifted. Shaking slightly, he tucked a strand of hair behind her ear.

"I need time," he rasped.

She understood, she really did. He'd been forced to walk away from everything he'd ever known, including the girl he'd planned to spend the rest of his life with. The shock of meeting his mate without time to adjust to all he'd lost couldn't be easy. But she couldn't shake the feeling that right now, in this moment, he would reject her if he could.

She nodded. "I know."

His throat bobbed then he pulled the door open, and they stepped inside.

EIGHT

BADEN

Dani dropped her helmet onto a low, grey couch and rested her hands on her hips. They stood in what looked like the lobby of a dance studio. Steel and glass end tables flanked the couch behind her, and a line of plastic chairs took up the wall opposite a long window overlooking the street where her bike, his rental, and several other vehicles were parked. The rest of the males had been waiting and fanned out around her like her own personal guard unit. Maybe they were. He was so far out of his element here, all he could do was study his surroundings to keep from staring at Dani.

She pointed to him then the four other males. "Baden, meet Connell, Finley, Pep, and William."

He nodded as they all exchanged a quick handshake.

"I'm going to change." She stepped toward a door to the right, pointing to one at the opposite end of the room. "Conn, you and Fin take him in the back and show him the computer room. I'll meet you there after the class. Pep, I need you to take his rental car back after you clear the camera and tracker." Her lips twitched into a smile as her eyes met Baden's. "And have your dad get William's bike out of storage. Baden will be borrowing it while he's here." She flicked her attention to the male beside Connell. "If that's all right with you, of course."

William grinned. "Fine by me."

Baden watched her disappear then turned to face the other males. Connell ticked his head, and they all followed the tall blonde through the door and into what was indeed a dance studio. Trophies lined a ledge along one wall, and a mirror stretched floor to ceiling opposite. The back was lined with more chairs and several more doors. The building didn't look this big from the front, and Baden glanced behind him toward the lobby.

"How big is this building?" He followed Finley across the large room, his shoes clacking against the hardwood floors.

"The whole thing was originally two separate structures. We built the studio space between them." Connell waved to the arched ceiling of the studio as he opened a door. "The computer room is in the lower level of the house. There are two flats, I think you'd call them apartments, upstairs. Finley and Pep live there full time. You'll be staying with them while you're here."

Connell led the way down a short hallway to another large room. The temperature change chilled his skin as he took in the layout.

Four computer workstations, each outfitted with two wide, curved monitors took up two of the long walls. At the back of the room two office doors stood open with additional workstations. No windows.

Pep stopped beside him. "I'll need the keys to the car so I can clear it and bring back the bike."

He handed over the keys, then watched the young male exit back into the studio. Dani's voice filtered through the door as she welcomed her students. Everything in his body wanted to go to her, but he couldn't get Leis out of his mind. He needed to know she was safe before he could let himself accept the reality of his mate on the other side of that door.

"How secure is this space?" he asked Connell. "Anyone can walk through that door."

All three of the males stiffened as Connell halted. "We've been doing this a long time, friend." He gave a grim smile. "No one gets through that door without an access key." He tapped the phone in his pocket. "RFiD and NFCs for every door. The codes and frequencies are rotated automatically."

Baden blinked and had to admit they'd taken more precautions than he expected. "Are there other access points besides that door?" He pointed to the studio.

"Emergency exit there, but it can't be opened by anyone from the outside." William pointed to the office on the left. "Access to the flats is at the back of the building. There is no external entry to this area except through the dance studio. The lower level we're standing in looks like a solid stone foundation."

Finley leaned a hip on one of the desks. "So, you're the mole?"

The male wore an earpiece, the corn snaking into the collar of his shirt barely noticeable against his light skin and fair hair.

Baden's jaw clenched. "I suppose I am."

A familiar cell phone tone chimed, and Baden instinctively reached for his back pocket and the phone that wasn't there. Disconnect hit him like a punch to the gut as Finley raised his cell to read a message.

He tapped the earpiece and pushed off the desk, striding toward the computer at the far end of the room. "Emerick has them. They just left the hotel in Chicago."

Them. *Leis and Koen.* He followed Finley to the workstation, watching as he unlocked the workstation with his fingerprint and pulled up a secure window. The downloading text didn't look familiar, the symbols elegant with accents and combined letters. *Gaelic.* Finley spoke quietly, his words almost lilting. Speech to text scrolled his reply before he sent the reply and locked the station with his fingerprint.

"We have tracking on the car, and we're tapped into the cameras at their Compound." Finley said as he pushed back from the computer. "We'll be able to keep a visual on everyone. Emerick will check in with us as soon as he gets the chance."

The two of them had been alone for more than 48 hours. Had Leis read the letter he gave her? Would they wait to bond, or had they already? He rubbed his forehead. He still needed to eat, and the five-hour time difference was starting to catch up to him.

"That's some code you wrote," Connell leaned on the desk next to Finley, drawing Baden from his spiraling thoughts. "We've been trying to get into your system for almost a decade."

"My grandmother insists on being thorough." Baden crossed to one of the computers, needing space from how carefully the male was watching his every expression. His eyes drifted across the desk until his gaze caught on the small silver box below the monitor. He tapped the etched logo on top. "These were built by her. How did you get them?"

"You're not the only one helping us." Dani's echo skidded across his skin. He turned to watch her cross the room. She'd changed to snug leggings and a loose grey t-shirt. She stopped next to him, and he followed the movements of her fingers as she wound her hair and pinned it to the back of her head. "Emerick and Ellen were able to get someone on the inside years ago. They are less conspicuous than you would have been."

"Andrew." Baden exhaled. "He said he met with Ellen."

"All eyes were on you and Leis," Dani's brow furrowed when he tensed. "Emerick will keep her safe," she said quietly, and he nodded.

"I believe you." He wasn't sure he did, but the conviction in her voice wound through him as she edged closer. Frustration at his helplessness made his skin feel tight. He resisted leaning toward Dani and

"What do you need me to do?"

Connell shrugged. "Until we get word from Emerick - nothing. You're supposed to be laying low."

His back teeth came together, and he felt Dani's attention lock onto him. He tried to slow his breathing. Being angry was irrational and he knew it, but being sent away to hide halfway around the world to keep him out of the way was insulting. He could do something and was about to say so when Finley pushed his chair back, the wheels grating against the concrete floor.

"They're at the Compound," Finley said and stood. "Everything else is already in place."

Baden frowned. "What's in place?"

Finley lifted a brow. "Didn't Ellen give you the information?"

It must have been in the tablet she'd given him on the plane. He'd been so focused on getting here, he hadn't taken the time to read over it. He crossed his arms, fighting down burning at the back of his throat. He was useless and ignorant.

"He hasn't had time to read the files." Dani inched even closer, and he resented the soothing tones in her echo though it softened the edges of his anger. She looked up at him, and he was glad to see nothing but honesty in her eyes. "Once we get word from Emerick, we will confront your grandmother."

"Confront her how?" Anger turned to fear, and the question ground out of him.

Dani paused, her eyes narrowing. Her echo flattened, almost disappearing as she replied, "There's a large group of Vampir gathering from around the world that will be arriving in Arizona over the next few days. Ellen and Emerick have been coordinating them for years."

Connell gestured to Finley. "When Emerick tells us it's time, we'll send them all to the compound."

Dani's echo smoothed further. "We have plenty of time to bring you up to speed."

He flicked his gaze between them. "Stop trying to calm me down and tell me what's going on."

William sighed, rolling his eyes. "Instead of growling at each other, why don't Conn and I get you settled upstairs? It was a long flight, and we've all had a bit of a shock." He raised a brow and glanced pointedly between him and Dani. "Nothing else is happening tonight. Everything will look better after food and sleep."

Baden drew a deep breath. The male was right, and a quiet place to think might get his head straight. "Fine."

NINE

Baden followed Conn and William out through the studio door, stalking away from her without a backward glance. She swallowed as the door latched shut then ran a hand down her face. The desire to comfort him, even to just stand close to him, had nearly overwhelmed her. She could help him regulate the emotions, but he was so filled with anger and fear, her mate radiated a warning not to come close. The food and sleep would hopefully give him a better perspective for tomorrow.

With a sigh, she took her seat at the workstation across from Fin and logged in. They still needed to finalize a few of the visas and plane tickets organized for the ones flying into the states from Europe and Asia, and she desperately needed the distraction from the male upstairs.

As her fingers raced over the keys, her mind wandered back to the odd undertones in his scent. The foulness was a such odds to the way he carried himself. The anger and fear she understood. Those emotions deepened the sharpness of allspice and the earthiness of the rosemary in his scent, natural responses to stress. But it was the sourness of the tobacco, normally the richly layered top note, the one that defined his inner belief about himself, that concerned her most.

It felt almost as if he hated himself. She paused her typing. Who had made him feel that way? Her hands shook as indignation on his behalf flooded her. She hoped it was his grandmother and not Leis. How could he care so much about someone who made him doubt himself? She resumed typing, sending the final confirmations to the individual Vampir who'd confirmed their reservations.

"Typing harder doesn't make the network faster." Fin pushed back from his desk, twisting to watch her. "And it won't make him less of an ass," he muttered under his breath.

She whirled on him. "When you've had everything you ever believed in destroyed right in front of you, tell me you wouldn't be a bit of an ass." She huffed. "Well, more of one than you already are."

"Fair enough." Fin flashed her a grin, his pale blue eyes sparkling. "Defending him already, are you? Other than taking a shot at Conn, has he even acknowledged what you are?"

"As best he can." She folded her arms.

"As best he can?" Fin mocked. "He should be doing everything he can to get you alone, but he's acting as if meeting his mate is no great event. What kind of male does that?"

Even though she'd scented the desire on Baden the moment he realized who she was, and though she knew there was more to his behavior than the other males would have picked up on, Fin's observations stung.

"He needs time." She stood and crossed to the small fridge for a bottle of water. Opening it, she leaned against the wall. "Did you read his file? His grandmother is a monster. It's no wonder he's cautious."

"Call it what you want." Fin turned back to his monitor. "If you were my mate, I wouldn't have walked away from you like that."

Taking a long swallow of the water, she glanced toward the ceiling and the flat Baden would be staying in. Under normal circumstances, Fin wasn't wrong. A male Vampir could be absolutely relentless when it came to claiming their mate. But these weren't normal circumstances.

Fin logged out and pushed away from his desk to study her, his expression thoughtful.

"What?" She asked.

"What happens if it's not a good match?" He asked quietly.

Before she could answer, Pep came through the studio door. "The bike is out front." He tossed the keys to her. "I fueled it up on the way back."

"Thank you, Pep." She tucked the keys in her pocket, and glanced at Fin. "It's a good match. We just need time."

"I hope so, friend," he said, then followed Pep back out the front, leaving her alone.

She dropped into a chair, pressing the heels of her hands into her eyes. Everything for the event back home was going according to plan, and meeting Baden was a surprise she'd not been prepared for, but Fin's question rattled her.

There were few bondings in the past decade, and the ones she knew about were all good. But what would happen if they didn't get along? Tears pricked her eyes as the door to the studio opened again. Twisting away to hide her face, she pretended to pick up a speck of dirt from the floor.

"Where's Fin?" Conn crossed to the workstation and logged in.

"I think he went with Pep to get something to eat." She rose and tossed the empty water bottle in the trash. Meeting Conn's concerned eyes, she huffed. "Don't you start."

"Start what?" He frowned. "What did Fin say?"

She shook her head. "The same thing everyone's thinking."

"And what would that be?" Conn leaned back in the chair, crossing his ankles.

"My mate doesn't want me."

"What? He said that?" Conn lifted half out of his chair. "He had no right..."

She held up a hand. "He didn't use those words, but we both

wonder if it's a bad match." Staring at the floor, she swallowed hard. "Ellen said he was...complicated."

Conn's bark of laughter startled her. "He's not as complex as he wants everyone to believe."

Her heart thudded against her ribs. "Did he say something to you or William?"

"Nothing directly, but he asked a lot of questions about you." He shrugged. "Well, he asked about your coding and where we were all from, but he listened with focus when we told him about you." Conn ticked his chin toward the ceiling. "William is getting him set up in the spare bedroom after he nearly fell asleep in his soup. He'll be better in the morning." He checked his watch. "Probably more like tomorrow afternoon."

She checked hers, surprised to note it was after midnight. With no windows, time held little meaning in the computer room until you were too tired to see anymore.

"When was the last time you ate?" Conn asked, logging into the computer.

"Right before I rode back here." She turned back to her own screen and pulled up the secure link to the compound. "I'll get something once this scan is done."

"It's after 7PM in Arizona. The tracker indicates they made it to the Compound, and they are all inside. We probably won't know anything else until tomorrow." He ticked his head toward the couch in the far office. "You should grab a few hours of sleep."

She wanted to argue but couldn't stifle a yawn.

He chuckled. "I'll finish the scans. Go. Like I said, everything will be better in the morning."

Glancing once more at the screen, she sighed, the adrenaline from all that had happened in the last few hours had worn off, leaving her limbs and eyelids heavy. Besides, he was right. Nothing else was liable to come out of the Compound tonight, and tackling all the work still ahead of them would be easier if she could sleep.

She stood and stretched. "Wake me if you see anything strange?"

"No promises."

He pulled a pair of headphones over his head as she crossed to the office and closed the door behind her. Kicking off her shoes and flicking on a lamp beside the couch, she stretched out on it and tucked one of the throw pillows behind her head. She stared at the ceiling where her mate slept above her for a long while before sleep finally pulled her under.

The computer room was empty when she opened the door the next morning. Twisting her hair into a knot atop her head, she settled into a chair and logged into her computer. Notices of receipts from the Vampir she'd sent confirmations to popped into her notifications, and she left the computer to finish downloading, crossing the room for a bottle of water.

As she cracked it open, William came in through the studio door carrying a take-out bag that smelled of sausage and fried potatoes.

"Good morning." He held the bag out to her. "Conn brought home some lunch. I figured you needed it more than me."

She took the offered food and yawned. "I didn't hear him leave. How late was he here?"

"He said he watched until about 3AM." He sipped from the tea mug in his other hand. "Then Baden woke up and came downstairs. They went to the pub down the street for breakfast." Her heart jumped at his name, making William grin. "They ate, dropped off the food, and then Conn took him out for a tour of the area."

She checked her watch, startled to realize it was already so late in the day. She ticked her head toward the office she'd slept in. "Did you eat?"

He shook his head. "I figured you might like the company."

They moved aside the laptop and settled across from one another at the small table. They ate in companionable silence until a chime sounded.

William started to rise, but she was already out of the office and logging into her computer. He followed, rolling the other desk chair across the room to sit beside her.

"Was that a message?" He pointed to an indicator flashing at the bottom of the screen.

"Yes. It looks like it came from the phone Leis has." She opened the messaging app.

L - Your grandmother is challenging Koen. I wish you were here.

DANI GLANCED AT WILLIAM. "Should we respond?"

"She'll think it's from Baden."

"I know." She bit her lip. "He would want her to know he's okay."

Conn made a non-committal sound. "He would, but can we risk it?"

She checked the monitors and cameras in the main living areas of the Compound. The only movement was from servants cleaning and preparing lunch.

Her fingers flew over the keyboard. "A single message to her will be secure."

B - I got your message.

SHE CHEWED HER LIP. "Did they separate her from Koen?"

William nodded. "They are staying in the same wing of the Compound, but his room is constantly under guard." He settled closer, his brow furrowed. "Can you connect their phones without using the network?"

"Only if they are close enough to each other." She adjusted the settings and studied the locations.

Leis was in the large common area with Res and another male, and Koen was in his room.

"I can't risk messaging Leis anything else. She's never alone. But I can send one to Koen." She typed quickly. "I'll see if I can find out how much time we have."

B - Just landed in Ireland. There are many of us coming. Keep texts to emergencies only. It won't take them long to figure out we are in the system. How long until Res forces a decision?

K - Two challengers, five more days.

She typed quickly, neither of them looking up as the studio door opened. "It looks like Koen has some freedom to move around the Compound. Maybe he can learn something we can't see."

B - Make allies if possible.

"Five days isn't much time." William frowned. "We'll need to be sending Baden back in a day or two. Otherwise, he won't be there in time."

CHAPTER

TEN

BADEN

A good night's sleep and a long motorcycle ride through the Irish countryside cleared his head. The scenery surrounding the studio was beautiful, and Conn assured him there was nothing else they needed to do, but it didn't alleviate the feelings of utter uselessness that haunted him.

They pulled up in front of the building and as Conn dismounted his bike, his cell phone chirped.

"This is Conn."

Baden ignored him, swinging his leg over the bike, then leaning on the machine to stare down the road where Dani had roared into his life. Even a day later, the memory of hearing her voice that first time still tightened the base of his spine. He rubbed a hand over his chest, trying to ease the strange ache spreading along his ribs.

"It's Ellen." Conn approached, holding the cell out to him.

For a heartbeat, he stared at the phone, unsure of what he would say to her, or if he even wanted to say anything. He glanced up, meeting Conn's gaze. The male raised a brow, extending the device further.

"You need to talk to her." He encouraged.

Sighing through his nose, he took the offered phone and lifted it to his ear.

"This is Baden."

"I only have a few minutes before my flight leaves," her echo smoothed over his skin, and he resented the way it immediately eased some of the tension. "I wanted to make sure you are all right."

"Why didn't you tell me?" He turned his back on Conn who stepped away.

"What didn't I tell you?" she asked.

"You should have told me she was my mate," he rasped.

"I could have been wrong," she said, the smile obvious in her tone. "I didn't want to give either of you false hope. We weren't sure about any of you, but I'm glad we were correct."

He clenched his teeth. He'd felt the same way when he'd encouraged Leis to spend time with Koen. The moment he'd realized she wasn't his, he hoped Koen was. A hope that had proven true, but that hope had torn his last relative from him.

"Baden." Wistfulness and sorrow flooded her echo. "I know trusting us with Leis has been hard for you, but she is where she is most needed. And so are you."

The ache in his chest thrummed, and he pressed the heel of his hand against it. "Is she okay?"

"She is. Are you in any pain?" Ellen asked quietly.

How could he answer that? "Everything hurts."

"This is important, Baden." There was a shuffle and murmuring, then her voice took on a hollow tone as if in a tunnel. "Do you feel physical pain right now?"

"Yes." The ache sharpened. "In my chest." The backs of his eyes burned. "What is happening?"

The smile was back in her voice. "The Blood Need. It's good that it's hit you so quickly."

"What is good about this?" He fought back the need to shout at her, as he heard more shuffling and her muffled 'thank you' to someone near her. "I don't understand. I don't know why I'm here."

"You do, you're just afraid to admit it," she chided. "Don't let your fear keep you from claiming your mate, child." Her echo grew stern. "You'll be returning to the states within days. If you leave there without bonding to her the pain for both of you will be…" She sighed. "It will be more than you need to endure."

"So, I'm supposed to bond to a female I just met, without any time to get to know her or her me?" His heart thrashed against the idea. "A complete stranger?"

"Does her voice feel like a stranger to you?"

No. She sounds like home. He shut down that thought. "Yes." He threaded a hand through his hair. "She's so completely different from…" he sighed.

"From Leis," Ellen finished for him. "Of course she is. Jordan is your mate, Leis is not. You know that."

His eyes stared unseeing into the distance as he replayed the last moments he'd been physically close to Leis and the wrongness that had coated his skin as he'd touched her. But just breathing the same air as Dani and listening to her speak; he couldn't deny the way the simple caress of her echo soothed the broken parts of him.

"I do," he admitted, rubbing his chest once more. "Is that why this hurts?"

"Yes." Ellen replied. "She needs you as much as you need her. I'm encouraging you not to wait before bonding. You'll have the rest of your lives to figure out everything the else."

"But why…"

"I am so sorry I don't have more time, but I truly have to go." She cut him off. "The plane is getting ready to take off. I will see you in Arizona in a few days." Her echo strengthened. "Trust each other and everything else will take care of itself. Promise me."

He clenched his teeth, then sighed. "I will try."

"All I can ask. See you soon."

The call ended and he dropped his hand to his side. Though his heart didn't want to admit it, he knew Ellen was right. Leis was with Koen, exactly where she should be. The girl he'd loved to this point in his life had found her true mate, and it wasn't him. He turned his head slightly to look at the glass front of the studio.

His mate was waiting for him inside. Dani wasn't like Leis; different from the soft-spoken girl he grew up with in a hundred different ways. The female inside the studio heated his blood in ways he hadn't even known were possible. He ran a hand down his face and turned to find Conn watching him. He held out the phone.

"Thank you," he said, tucking his hand back in his pocket. "Tell me about Dani?"

Conn folded his arms and hummed. "She's hotheaded, rides that bike like the devil's in her back pocket, and dances like her feet are on fire." The male cocked his head. "And she's as shocked as you are."

"I'm leaving to go back to the states soon." Baden toyed with the seam of his jean pocket. "Ellen told me we - Dani and me - should bond as soon as possible."

Conn's boots scuffed on the sidewalk as he leaned onto his bike and crossed his legs. "I've been told it changes everything, but it's certainly nothing I have any experience with."

"What should I do?" Baden asked.

"You dance?"

His lip drew upwards. "I do." A car door shut, both he and Conn turning to watch Fin and Pep approach. "When I started, I never thought I would be any good at anything besides computers."

"What else are you good at?" Fin asked.

He matched Conn's grin. "Dance."

"Well, let's find out how good you are." Fin crossed the sidewalk and held the door open. "I'll get the others."

Baden entered the empty dance studio and paused in the middle of the room, Conn a few steps behind him as Fin disappeared into the computer room to get Dani and William. His skin tightened in anticipation. He could do this. Dancing helped him relax. Usually.

"So, what style did you train in?" Conn asked.

He shook out his hands and turned toward him and Pep. "Couples freestyle. Impromptu was always a class favorite. We studied a bit of everything then twice a month the instructor drew names for random pairs." He glanced down at his boots. "Though these are not going to work."

Pep gestured toward a row of lockers. "We'll find a pair of shoes that will fit you. You and Fin are probably the same size."

He was finishing tying the laces when Dani came through the door. His hands froze as he watched her cross the dance floor. He hadn't seen her since last night, and she'd changed into a pair of black leggings and a short sleeved cut off top that barely covered the top of her hips. As if she'd anticipated the dance, she wore black slippers with a strap across the top of her foot.

She looked as nervous as he felt, and the air in the room charged with anticipation and amusement from the other males. She paused a few feet away, resting her hands on her hips.

"Fin says you wanted to dance?" Her echo conveyed her disbelief, and he huffed a laugh.

"Fin gave me little choice."

She raised a brow. "Well, Fin?"

The male stood before the sound system a wry grin on his face. "Mr. America here says he likes impromptu freestyle." He glanced between them and Baden's hands tightened. "Let's start with something easy." He nodded to the center of the floor. "You two just going to stand there?"

His stomach tightened as Dani chewed her lower lip. As the first notes of the song filtered through the speakers he extended a hand to her. "West coast?" Her chin lowered and the slow up curve of her mouth sent every thought out of his head.

"My favorite." Her hand landed in his and he tugged her into the easy back and forth glide of the swing.

The dance style was designed for the man to lead the woman up and down the dance floor in a single line, encouraging her to display her grace, playfulness, and balance. He did his best to oblige, and following the steady beat of the music, he sent her to the end of their outstretched arms. The smooth arc of her body as she moved stole the breath from him.

The lithe sway of her hips and the gentle curve of her shoulders as she undulated to the music sent images flashing through his mind that he wasn't ready to process. He stumbled as he drew her back toward him, but managed to sidestep in time to avoid tripping her.

Lifting and rotating his arm, he gave her the space to rise to her toes and spin, intending to catch her opposite hand as she passed behind him, but when her fingers grazed his lower back, he stumbled again. As they fell back into the basic steps, her eyes met his. Concern, then heat flared across her expression, and he was sure she scented the desire raging through him.

He closed his eyes and reached behind her to give her the space to pass in front of him as she spun again, but as her body brushed his he couldn't resist letting his palm slide across the curve of her waist. His entire body went rigid, then liquid as the echo from her sigh sent fire down his spine. They fumbled through the last measures of the song, then stepped apart. He couldn't look at her. He'd danced like a novice.

"All right." Fin intoned. "That was less than stellar. Let's try something else."

ELEVEN

By the third song, a fast waltz, she was practically flying in Baden's arms. After the heat of desire settled to a manageable flare, they had both regained their poise and their bodies moved in tandem as if they'd been training together all their lives. The walls and the floor spun by as the fell into the lope of the waltz and his warm hands skimmed her hips and waist as she spun and whirled as he led them through a series of turns. Never faltering their feet moved in unison and she never wanted the music to stop.

As the song rose to the crescendo, he sent her spinning then caught her in a deep dip, that had her clinging to his powerful shoulders to keep from falling to the floor. The song ended and the room was silent except for their panting breaths. For long heartbeats, she gazed up into the rich texture of his dark eyes until his dropped to her lips, and his breath shuddered. The scent of him filled her lungs with a need so strong she pressed her tongue against the roof of her mouth as her fangs threatened to rip free. Grasping for control, she rested a palm on his chest, marveling at the heart pounding in time with hers.

"Baden?" She rasped.

He blinked, then swung her upright, but didn't let go. "Are you all right?"

She couldn't stop the giggle that escaped. "Fine. I'm fine."

His throat bobbed and as he shifted closer she wet her lips in anticipation. The movement seemed to startle him, and he stiffened his arms to put space between them. He glanced around the room, then relaxed. She followed his gaze, realizing the others had slipped out at some point. A glance out the window revealed all their vehicles were gone. They were completely alone.

"I — I need to talk to your brother." He ran his palms down her arms, then took a step back.

The absence of his warmth was startling, and she shook out her hands, unsure what had just happened. "I can call him. But why?"

"It's custom in our Clan to ask for our mate's family for a blessing." He reached up to tuck a strand of hair behind her ear.

"Oh." She looked over her shoulder. "We can use one of the offices."

He nodded and followed her to the door leading to the computer room. His smile seemed forced as nervousness flooded his scent. "Where does he live?"

"My family owns a farm in Illinois." After the warmth of the studio, the cool air of the offices skittered along her skin. "We lease the land to a family who raise cattle."

Flipping on the lights, she tugged two chairs in front of a workstation and logged in. "He might not be home." She checked her watch. "The two of us run a dance studio in Chicago."

"He's a dancer?" Baden sat, rolling his chair close enough his arm brushed hers.

"He is." She smiled as the video call attempted to connect. "He's the lead choreographer for..."

"Dani?" Zane answered, but the screen remained blue. "What's wrong?" His worried tone made her grin.

"Nothing is wrong," Dani replied. "Turn on the camera."

She bit her lip as shuffling and muttered curses filtered through.

"Stupid computers." Glancing at Baden, he bit his lips closed against a laugh.

"Just click on the —" she started to say, then Zane's scowling face lit up the screen. "There you are." Her heart tightened at the concern lining his face as he studied her. His hair was mussed as if he'd raked his fingers through it, and a bit of mascara smudged below his right eye. He looked tired. And worried.

"You're okay?" He asked. "Everything's okay?"

"I'm fine," she assured him. Beside her, Baden made a choked sound, and she turned to him.

"Parish." His eyes flicked between her and the screen. "Zane Parish is your brother?"

She frowned. "Yes."

"As in, Zane Parish of In The Arena?" Baden blinked then shook his head. "No wonder you're so good."

"No. No. No." Dani dropped her head back to look at the ceiling. "Please don't fawn over him. His ego is big enough." She sighed dramatically as Baden choked on a laugh.

"Am I missing something?" Zane asked, brows raised almost to his hair line. "Because I feel like I'm missing something."

"Zane, meet Baden." She waved her hand between the screen and the male beside her. "Baden, meet my brother, the *not*-superstar-dancer, Zane."

"Oh yes I am," he automatically retorted, his eyes twinkling as they shifted to Baden who looked ready to puke. "It's nice to meet you." Zane frowned. "Are *you* okay?"

"I'm good." He flicked a glance at her, then drew a breath. "I'm just not sure where to begin this conversation."

Zane cocked his head, as if confused, then his eyes widened and locked onto hers. She fought back a grin and gave a subtle nod, along with a narrowing of her eyes. *Don't taunt him.* Zane's answering grin as he settled back in his chair was not reassuring.

Baden cleared his throat. "I asked Dani to call you —"

"Jordan. We call her Jordan." Zane interrupted.

They absolutely did not. She was going to throttle him when she got home.

Baden blinked and tried again. "I asked Jordan to call you because —"

"Do you have intentions toward my sister?" Zane interrupted again, the twinkle in his eyes telling her he was enjoying this far too much.

Oh, he was in so much trouble.

"Well, yes." Bewildered, Baden glanced at her. "It is custom in my Clan to ask her nearest relative —"

"Shouldn't it be the oldest —"

"Zane!" She hissed, her cheeks heating. "Stop it."

He bit his lips, his shoulders hunching in a held back laugh then he straightened, leaning forward to rest his forearms on the desk. "I'm sorry, sis." He looked to Baden. "Are you her mate?"

Baden eased a breath. "I am."

Zane's expression turned serious, and she forgot how badly she'd wanted to choke him as he asked, "Do you promise to take care of her and protect her and our family as long as both of you live?"

Baden's throat bobbed. "To the best of my ability, yes."

Zane's eyes slid to hers. "He's your mate?"

"Yes," she whispered.

He held her gaze. "You want my blessing?"

"We do." She reached for Baden's hand, and he wove their fingers together.

Zane looked back and forth between them one more time, silver lining his lower lashes. "Then I gladly give it." As a tear slid down his cheek, he swiped at it, lengthening the smudge of mascara toward his temple. "Look what you've done." He leaned forward, using his pinky to remove the smear. "I thought this stuff was waterproof," he muttered.

Dani choked a laugh, covering her face with a hand as Baden watched, wistfulness and sorrow creeping into his scent. She squeezed his hand. He squeezed back.

"I look forward to meeting you when you both get back to the states," Zane said.

"I'll bring her home as soon as I can," Baden said.

Zane grinned. "Congratulations."

"Thank you," she and Baden replied at the same time.

"I would like to speak to my sister for a moment, if you don't mind."

Baden rose, tightening his grip once before letting go. "I'll wait in the other office."

TWELVE

BADEN

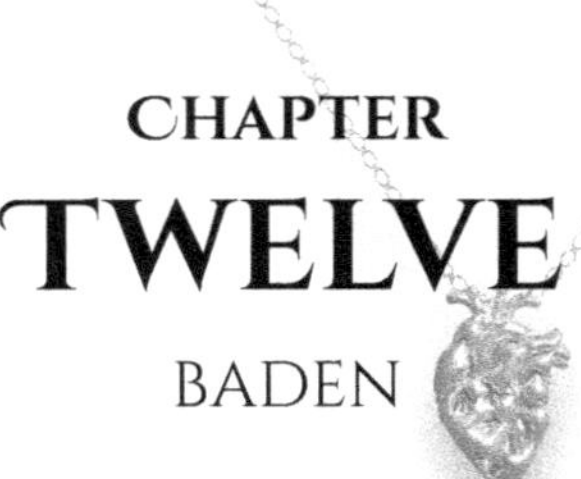

Baden left Dani still talking to her brother. He numbly crossed the main room and walked into the other office, not bothering to turn on the lights. He lowered into a chair in front of the workstation and clicked the keyboard. The screen lit up with a security login. With a few keystrokes, he bypassed the main screen and hacked in using the back door code he'd implanted in case this team had turned out to be a problem.

As he navigated the operating system, he let the banter between Dani and her brother play through his mind. His mate was Zane Parish's sister. He'd followed the male's career for years. Even tried to emulate some of his routines. But her brother's stardom wasn't what bothered him.

For years, he and Leis had shared the kind of relationship Zane and Dani obviously had. He and Leis had joked, teased, and laughed together, sharing inside jokes, shared glances, and relaxed moments just enjoying each other's company.

The pain in his chest twanged, and he pressed his hand against it. It felt like his heart was breaking all over again. He missed Leis, and while he'd danced with Dani, he hadn't worried about her safety one time.

The challenge would be underway, and he had to know Leis was okay.

THIRTEEN

"Earth to Dani," Zane said.

She ignored him and watched Baden walk away, drinking in the fluid strength of his movements and admiring the way his dress pants accentuated his backside.

Zane's continued attempts to get her attention only made her that much more determined to ignore him as long as possible. Even without meeting in person, it was clear the two of them would get along. Good thing, given the fact that she and her brother were practically inseparable.

A loud scraping sound from the speaker made her flinch.

"Hello? Is this still on?" Zane taunted.

She was tempted to disconnect the call but instead shot him a glare that turned into a puff of laughter. He leaned close to the camera, and the only thing she saw was his giant hazel eyeball staring out at her.

They both cracked up when she jabbed a finger at the camera on her side, making him involuntarily jerk back.

"Wow. Self-preservation is a real thing." He rubbed a finger over his eyelid, slightly smearing his mascara and eyeliner, then sat back in his chair. "I'm really happy for you, sis. Is he any good?"

"Ask me tomorrow," she replied and wriggled her brows before covering her rapidly heating face. "Did I just make that joke to my brother?"

Zane chuckled. "Yeah, you did." His cheeks pinked. "I probably should have worded that better. Can he dance?"

"We haven't had much time in the studio, but yeah." Her heart sped up. "He can dance."

"Not as good as me though, right?"

"No." She rolled her eyes. "You are still the reigning diva of dance."

"Good to know." He sobered and rolled forward. "When are you coming home?"

"Not for another two weeks." She let her head loll back on the chair. "I have to stay here and monitor the network until we get the all clear from the States."

Which meant tonight would be the only night she and Baden would have together until he flew home. Anticipation fluttered in her stomach, and the memory of his strong hands guiding her across the dance floor made her squirm in the chair. It squeaked, drowning out what Zane said.

"Did I –"

Squeak.

"Did I tell you –"

Squeak. Squeak.

"Yesterday, I —"

Squeak. Squeak.

Zane caught on. "DidItellyouIgotacat?"

She laughed. "What?"

"I found a cat." He lifted the tiniest, fluffiest ball of tan fur she'd ever seen. "Her name is Apple." He held her close to the camera.

"Aww." Dani leaned closer, then startled back when the kitten hissed at the screen.

Zane laughed and scratched her between the ears. "Burnt Apple Fritter, to be exact." He set the puff ball aside and held up a hand to the camera. It was crisscrossed with tiny scratches. "Dad would be proud. I haven't cussed at her."

The mention of her dad made Dani's throat clench and the backs of her eyes stung.

"I'm sorry." Zane's shoulders slumped, and he sighed. "I wish he could have been here."

She swallowed against the tightness in her throat and nodded. He would have loved Baden immediately.

"I know he would be proud of you," Zane said quietly. "Mom too."

Her brother's face blurred but she blinked away the tears and forced a smile. "How's Zachary adjusting to driving himself to school?"

Zane gave her a knowing look but let the deflection slide. "The van is still in one piece, though the front end will need an alignment. He likes to cut corners."

"Sounds like him," she said wistfully. "I miss you guys."

"You'll be home soon enough." Zane disappeared then came back with the kitten tucked under his chin. He looked happier than she'd seen him in months until the cat batted at his nose, claws out. "Toaster strudel! You need to learn some manners."

She huffed a small laugh then glanced over her shoulder. "I need to go. Fin and Con need my help before Baden and I...well...before I take the night off." Heat prickled the back of her neck. Zane's smirk didn't ease her nerves. "What?"

"You're never off balance around a guy." He lifted a shoulder. "It's kind of amusing."

"Hanging up now." She reached for the screen.

"G'night, sis."

The screen's image resolved into a picture of the Dublin guys at the edge of one of Scotland's famous cliffs. One of the monitoring icons slowly faded from color to grayed out and back to color, indicating the filter was processing data. She frowned and glanced toward the workroom. Fin and Con had their heads close together studying a spreadsheet.

"Are you guys running a scan?" she called.

Fin looked over his shoulder. "No. It finished about twenty minutes ago. All clear." He straightened. "Is something thing wrong?"

"No," she said slowly and checked the icon. It was solid color. Not running. "Must have been an echo." She stood and stretched. "Do you need me for anything?"

Connell swiveled his chair to face her. "Ready for your hot date?"

Heat bloomed across her cheeks, and both men laughed.

"Congratulations." Con wagged his eyebrows as he returned his attention to the screen. "We won't wait up."

"Thanks," she mumbled and headed for the door.

Though the room was dark, movement in one of the side offices caught her eye. The faint glow of a negative screen outlined a familiar head and shoulders.

Baden must have stopped to check the scan before he left. She pocketed her bike keys and stepped silently into the office. His back was to her, and his shoulders hid most of the screen, but she saw enough to recognize the backdoor messaging protocol they'd installed for emergencies.

"Hey. What are you doing?"

Threads of ice tightened around her chest when his fingers snapped across the keyboard, blacking out the screen. She inhaled, sure she would be able to read him, but instead, her senses slammed against his fear and a sour note of shame.

"What's going on?" She tried to keep the accusation out of her echo but failed. In the faint light, she watched his Adam's apple bob. "Baden?" she prompted.

When he didn't answer or look around, she turned the chair with a shove of her foot.

His hands clenched the arm rests and the line of his jaw flexed, but his eyes stayed on the floor. She opened her mouth to demand he answer but jerked back when the office door banged open and Fin stormed inside.

"We just intercepted a message to..." His eyes jumped from Baden to the computer, to her, and back to Baden. "Did you send it?"

"I – I had to know..." Baden whispered roughly.

Silence hung in the air as the implications of his words hit them.

"Had to know what, exactly?" Fin enunciated each word as icy betrayal flooded her.

"Did you message her?" Dani's voice rasped, and she watched her pain hit him.

Baden's eyes squeezed closed, and he bobbed his head. "I'm sorry. I had to know." Shame and regret threaded through the air, but it was too late. He'd put all of their work in jeopardy.

"Do you have *any* idea what you've done?" Fin lapsed into a tirade of Celtic phrases no one needed a translator to understand and punched a monitor on his way out of the room. She and Baden flinched when it hit the floor.

When Baden finally looked up, the desperation in his eyes made her take a step back.

"I made sure no one can trace it." He let go of the chair and leaned forward with his elbows on his knees. His fingers twisted into his perfectly combed hair, leaving it sticking out in all directions in a way that normally would have made her want to tease him, but his next words stole anything amusing from the situation. "Leis is all I have left. I had to know she was all right."

Leis was all he had left? There was no lie in his scent. Cold settled all the way into her bones.

Dani took another step back. Less than an hour ago he'd asked Zane for permission to claim her. But Leis was still all he could think about? She let the ice she felt in her blood lace her echo.

"Well?" She gritted her teeth against the tears threatening to choke her. "Is she all right?"

He nodded.

"Good. Because I'm not."

His head jerked up, but she didn't want to see his face. The office door hit the wall with a satisfying bang as she stormed out. Eight heads swung her way. The spicy tang of Baden's shame hung in her nostrils as she bolted through the studio and out the front door where her Ducati waited just outside. The fresh air of a ride would clear her head, and she strapped the helmet on. She left the face shield down to hide her expression from Connell who charged out the door a few steps behind her.

"Hold on. You're in no mood to tangle with this machine," he warned but didn't stop her when she tossed her leg over and knocked the kickstand up. "At least let me –"

The growl of her bike's engine drowned out his cursing, and she sped away before he'd made it three steps to his own ride. It wouldn't take him long to catch her, and there was little doubt Baden would be right behind him.

Once she cleared the narrow alley, she glanced over her shoulder and barely caught a glimpse of Connell straddling his bike and Baden bursting out the back door.

In spite of the pain, a thrill shot through her and a grin spread across her face. She crouched low over the tank and opened the throttle, heading for her favorite spot.

Let them chase me.

FOURTEEN

BADEN

The cruiser's engine screamed in protest as he twisted the throttle in an attempt to catch Dani's Ducati and Connell's Suzuki, but it was no use. Even if his bike matched their straightaway speed, the sport bikes would out corner him. Frustration rippled into fear as the pair disappeared around the bend, both of them nearly dragging their knees on the pavement as the road twisted through the mist and down a hillside.

Barely remembering to roll off the brake to keep his front tire from locking up, Baden managed to take the turn without sliding the rear. The road straightened out, and his breath caught when he spotted Connell climbing off his bike a hundred yards away.

The rear tire skidded to a stop as Baden kicked the bike into neutral and killed the engine. Relief flooded him at the sight of Dani's bike resting on the kickstand instead of in the ditch.

"Where is she?" He searched the field, but she was nowhere in sight.

Connell removed and lowered his helmet. "She needed a ride to clear her head." He leaned a hip on the seat of his bike. "She won't go far."

Baden exhaled and slid his own helmet off. "Is she always like this?"

Connell barked a laugh. "She has her moments." His eyes darted to the white Ducati. "I don't know what 'appened between the two of you, but that bike isn't easy to keep up with when she's in the mood to open the throttle."

"You should have let me go after her. I would have caught her." Though Connell's ride was better suited to chasing her down, he was tired of always having an audience. His body tightened with the need to talk to her alone. "I would never let anything happen to her."

Connell picked at his nails. "It's no secret what you an' her are, but we can't forget she's still under my protection."

"Are you suggesting I would hurt her?" He stepped into the man's space, but Connell waved him off with a sneer.

"I ain't suggesting you're even capable of it. I followed her because we can't risk either of you, and she isn't exactly known for thinking straight when she's wired up." He smirked and flicked a hand up and down Baden's body. "And you, my friend, wire her up."

Baden huffed. "I doubt that."

Connell's laugh was loud. "You don't get it do you?"

"Get what?" he growled.

"She wants you more than anything, but she ain't gonna bite until she knows you trust her."

Fire crept up the back of Baden's neck. "Trust her? I shared everything I know! She told you herself I wasn't lying."

"Oh, you told us all about your fancy coding and proved you're willin' to take out that grandmother of yours." His voice deepened in warning. "But you need to admit you're still in love with the other girl."

Connell's words hit like a blow to the chest, nearly making him stumble back a step, but he held his ground. He opened his mouth, closed it, and swallowed hard as the other man raised a brow in challenge.

Was he still in love with Leis? He was. There was no way he could deny it.

The heart pounding against his ribs hadn't had time to heal from the loss of the girl he'd loved and protected for the first twenty-two years of his life. The betrayal on Dani's face when she saw what he'd been willing to risk for Leis spiked through him. He regretted compromising the new network, but he'd needed Leis to know he hadn't abandoned her. She was part of him. His head knew she was family, but the heart that had loved her for so many years wasn't easily convinced to stop.

"Leis is family," he said roughly. "It's not possible for me to love her that way." *It never was,* he thought angrily, though she was everything he'd been conditioned to want from the woman he would spend the rest of his life with. From the moment he was old enough to understand what it meant to be attracted to a women, he thought he wanted his intended to be Leis; cultured, soft-spoken, and feminine in dresses and high heeled sandals - until the leather clad, hotheaded, smart-mouthed Dani Parish tipped his entire world askew.

Every minute he was around her, the Blood Need tore through his veins with increasing power. It screamed at him to give her his blood, to let her taste him. And there was no denying the attraction between them. He dug the heel of a hand against his ribs as if the pressure would relieve the pain tearing his chest in two.

"Tell yourself that." The other male snorted. "For the record, that's not what bothers Dani. She understands your connection to the girl. But you can't keep lyin' about it. She can't compete with those kinds of memories, and she won't try."

"That's what no one seems to understand," Baden said roughly. "There is no competition." He walked to Dani's bike and rested a hand on the seat. "I didn't know it would be so overwhelming to want someone as badly as I want her." He made a fist when Connell snorted again. "It's not just her blood or her body." The admission made his face hot, but he met Connell's gaze squarely. "My life was very different than hers. There were a million rules for this kind of thing." He dropped his eyes to the sleek bike that was a stark contrast to the low-slung cruiser he preferred. "And I've never met anyone like her. I don't know what to do with how she makes me feel. She makes me want to be free and...wild..." he trailed off, surprised by his own words.

"And that's the bit that scares you, isn't it?"

Baden snapped his head up but read no taunting in the man's tone or on his face.

"Look." Connell crossed his arms and shrugged. "Dani grew up with fifteen brothers. There isn't much that scares her." He smirked. "Except you. She's been terrified ever since you showed up."

Baden scanned the field behind the other man, and his shoulders squared as understanding settled around him. How had he been so blind? The bikes themselves represented everything that was different between them. She rode with abandon, thriving on the adrenaline rush that came with pushing her control of the machine to the edge.

His breath left him in a rush as her reluctance to trust him suddenly made perfect sense. His fear of losing control led her to conclude he would want to control *her*. But it was her wildness that drove him crazy in all the best ways. She was everything he'd always wanted to be but was never allowed to even think about.

His focus cleared, and Connell's stance relaxed. The man was right. She did scare him, but scary was exactly what he needed. He dropped his chin, striding toward Connell and the barely visible path through the grass behind him as the tingle in his spine crept upward.

"Now you look like you're ready for a bite." Connell grinned and picked up his helmet. "I'll see you at the studio tomorrow."

Baden paused and clasped his outstretched hand. Connell looked down in surprise.

"She can't run if the bike won't start," Baden said as Connell pocketed the keys to the Ducati and tugged his helmet on. "I'll bring her home on mine."

He chuckled and swung a leg over his bike. "Pep and I will come get it later."

"Thank you," Baden replied, but the words were lost when Connell revved his bike and tore off down the road.

He scanned the field as he stepped onto the path. A few strides away, it sloped down toward a small pond of murky green water, and his heart clattered against his ribs when he spotted Dani skipping rocks across the surface.

FIFTEEN

Dani didn't turn when dirt crunched behind her. Baden's scent rode the wind ahead of him and made the roof of her mouth ache. The spicy bite of his shame lingered, but it mixed heavily with the rich sweetness of his determination to make things right. She pressed her tongue against the roof of her mouth and bent to select another smooth flat rock. She loosed it across the surface of the pond as Baden's steps halted beside her. His emotions crested over her like the ripples her stone left on the surface of the water. She picked them out with each skip of the rock. Regret, sadness, hope, and a thread of anticipation that made her jaw clench.

"I was three when Hayden and Stephanie took me in." Baden crouched and sorted through the pebbles at the water's edge. "I spent most of my time with Leis' brother, Andrew. He was my best friend."

Her defenses flared as the raw wave of his pain hit her. Though it somehow felt different than when she'd left him behind, she gritted her teeth against the draw to empathize with his pain.

"The two of us ran cross-country together and spent a lot of time in the hills around the compound." He straightened, but instead of tossing the rock he'd picked out, he extended his hand to her. "We ran every morning and talked about almost everything." Dark eyes swung her way, but they weren't focused on her. "Including our bonding ceremonies."

The hardness in his tone made her blink. Unsure how to respond, she took the rock, turning it over and over in her hand as he spoke.

"From the time Leis and I were pledged; her dad kept my family's crib stored away for our ceremony." The breeze flipped a lock of hair into his face, and he brushed it aside impatiently. "Our ceremony was planned for the week after we graduated high school. I was looking forward to it, if only to get us both out of her parents' house." He looked up, seeming to scan the sky for answers. "I didn't know why at the time, but I knew things weren't right. I hoped getting our own place would fix whatever was wrong with me."

She froze as a tremor went through him and then frowned. Leis was the one born with a defect not him. His voice remained steady, but the admission seemed to put a crack in his control. She opened her mouth to ask why he thought there was ever anything he could do, but he continued as if anticipating her questions.

"In public, everyone blamed Leis's lack of smell for the delay in our Bonding." His hands tightened to fists. "But grandmother told me if I truly wanted to be Bonded to her, then my scent and blood would heal her. I believed the reason Leis continued to suffer was because somewhere deep inside me, I didn't want to bond to her." His throat bobbed and he rubbed a palm over his heart. "And I couldn't admit to anyone she was right. I didn't."

"Did it hurt?" she asked softly. His eyes were like flint when they met hers. "When you touched her. Did it hurt?"

"Yes, but not as bad as it should have because we're so closely related." He rolled his shoulders and his gaze drifted past her in thought. "During our senior year, when the Blood Need should have been irresistible, I stayed away from the house for days at a time. I let them believe it was to keep us pure, but the longer it went on the more repulsed I was at the thought of being near her. I learned to hide it when we had to be together, and I denied the way I really felt because I truly loved her." He squeezed his eyes shut. "I thought it was all my fault we were suffering."

Dani silently cursed his grandmother. The frustrating thing was that the woman had been partially right. The male's scent and blood had the ability to heal, but only for his true intended. The mixture of the male and female blood after the bonding made them nearly impervious to aging, illness, or disease. Researchers were only now developing the technology to begin to understand how or why, but no amount of wishing would ever create such healing between a couple who could not bond.

Baden held out a hand, and she placed the rock in his palm. The breath left her in a puff when he caught her wrist and lifted it to his lips before letting go.

"Then, a few months before graduation, Hayden took me out to dinner and showed me the letters and records he found in the false bottom of the crib. Everything made sense." He notched the stone in the hollow of his forefinger and thumb before letting it fly across the water. It skipped over the surface in time with her heartbeats before disappearing beneath the surface. The corner of his mouth lifted, revealing a deep dimple in his cheek she'd never noticed before.

She held her breath as his expression hardened again and he tucked his hands in his front pockets. She wanted to take them in hers, but something held her back as he continued.

"Haydn discovered he and my father, Heinrich, were brothers, fraternal twins actually. My grandmother had them separated at birth to hide the fact that she was operating some kind of *breeding program*." His words sent a chill down her neck. "My grandmother knew all along Leis and I couldn't possibly be intended for each other." His brown eyes sparked like flint and the wall containing his emotions cracked, instantly souring his sweet scent with the bite of sulfur. She turned her head to cover the gag, but he was too lost in the memories to notice her reaction. "When my dad confronted her, she arranged to have him and my mother killed."

"Res was trying to force Leis and I to bond because children from our mother's blood lines were the only hope of keeping our DNA from completely deteriorating. She would have expected us to produce children by any means necessary." He swallowed hard and looked at her. "She saw us as a science experiment. But we were just kids." His voice broke, and so did his emotions. The air filled with the scent of wet burning leaves, strong enough to make her eyes water. "We had no clue — I — had no clue, and for the first eighteen years of my life, I spent every minute falling in love with the heart of a girl I expected to spend the rest of my life with. I thought there was something wrong with me because I couldn't love her the way they told me I should. If my dad hadn't written those letters…"

The confused and broken little boy in his eyes shattered her heart. She took his hand, realizing that, in a lot of ways, he was still that kid. He'd tried all his life to be what his family wanted but was never good enough. He'd been forced into an impossible relationship, while his own grandmother played them all like pawns in a sick game.

She swallowed against the ache in her throat for the boy he should have been. But he'd been forced to hold it all in to save the girl he'd loved and cared about his entire life until what he'd kept hidden was so foul he was genuinely afraid to let it out.

His normally sweet tobacco scent smelled rotten because this wound had festered inside him for years while he played a part. He'd endured the pain, the betrayal, and the loss without ever revealing to anyone what he knew. His abilities had been turned inside out, taught to hold things inside rather than changing the world around him.

She breathed deeply as rage boiled in her chest. She let it churn even as she shielded him from it. She didn't want him to misinterpret it and shut down again. Not when she was finally seeing the true Baden, the one who was forever hers.

How could she blame him for continuing to hide? He'd known nothing *but* hiding. Now, he needed to know he was safe with her. He would always be safe with her. Though the foulness of his scent should have made her back away, she stepped close.

"There is nothing wrong with you," she said softly. "To have gone through all of that and never lost hope...You are the strongest man I know." Tears burned the back of her throat. "I'm sorry I got upset with you for caring about her so much. I didn't understand." His Adam's apple bobbed, and his shoulders lowered. "But I want to, because I want to understand you."

His gaze flicked between her eyes, searching for the truth of her words. His brows pinched. "But you're still angry."

"Of course I am, but not at you." She let a bit of the rage into her echo and exhaled in relief when he shifted closer. "I'm angry *for* you."

His brown eyes pierced hers, and as he stepped into her, she noticed tiny lines of green threaded out from his inner irises like blades of grass pushing through rich soil. He slid a hand around her waist; his whole body shook with emotion and need as they met.

Gentle fingers threaded through her hair, and she leaned her cheek into his palm. His breath warmed the skin of her forehead, filling her nostrils with the smell of pipe smoke and incense. "Will you have me?"

She looked up as a flash of pain tore through the roof of her mouth, and the coppery tang of blood coated her tongue. His hand tightened at the small of her back when she winced. Then his gaze dropped to her lips. His pupils blew wide and the hand that cupped her cheek slid downward until his thumb caught her lower lip, softly pressing it downward to expose her fangs.

She kissed the pad of his thumb and felt his hitch of breath before he breathed her name.

Then his lips were on hers, and the world fell away. His breath filled her mouth as he spoke her name again and again. The desperation in his scent shot a jolt of desire through her strong enough to make her gasp, and she drew back.

It was happening too fast. She wanted to savor the seconds before her fangs sank into his lower lip.

He made a sound suspiciously like a growl, nearly making her knees buckle as his fingers dug into her hip and lower back, but she resisted his pull until he released her and stepped back. The absence of his hold nearly sent her stumbling backward into the pond. He steadied her but let go, balling his hand into a fist.

"I'm sorry." His hand shook as it threaded through his hair. "I don't know what I'm doing…"

"No. That's not what I meant." Dani caught his elbows, pulling him toward her. "Don't do that with me."

He swallowed hard, uncertainty bleeding through his scent. "Don't do what?"

She cupped his face. "Take all the blame on yourself. We'll be in this together from now on. You can't push me away when things get hard."

His hand slipped around her waist, smoothing up her back. "Tell me what you want from me." He exhaled, his gaze dropping to her lips. "Because all I can think about…"

She captured his next words in her mouth, sliding her hands into his perfectly combed hair and pulling him close.

It was all the encouragement he needed. He palmed the back of her neck, tilting her face and raking his tongue across her still descended fangs.

Color and passion exploded across her tongue. All the layers of emotion that made Baden the male he was flooded her senses, losing a small noise of surprise from deep in her chest as everything she thought she knew about bonding realigned into a powerful soul deep bond that both calmed and terrified her.

Baden stepped toward her, moving her backward until her shoulders met a tree and his body aligned perfectly with hers. She hadn't realized how much broader he was, and having his size wrapped around and over her made her body tense and loose all at the same time. His doubts about himself and their bonding raged against the desire and blood need driving him to claim her mouth with a fierceness that bordered on desperation. She fought the urge to break apart all the emotions pouring out of him, wanting desperately to soak in the way his body felt and the way his palms were warm against her skin. But the moment slid away, as the depth of his pain and fear threatened to overtake her.

His lips barely lifted from hers as he sucked in a breath before claiming her again. She allowed his deepest emotions to wash over her but instead, his thoughts grew shadowy and dark, violent places where memories and primal desires should have been nearly caused her to draw back in horror at what had been done to him.

Her childhood had been filled with laughter and love, surrounded by a huge family that would do anything for each other. Her heart shattered as she sensed the desertion he'd felt when his parents died, the fear and loathing he had for the female who'd twisted his gift into a weapon turned against himself. The flood of memories faded, and she sensed his control return. She gasped, trying to draw him closer, to offer him the acceptance and love he'd been denied, asking him not to shut her out.

SIXTEEN

BADEN

Baden's fingers quaked against her ribs as his hands trailed down her sides, and she arched against him wanting more. He eased back, pressing his thumbs against her hips to still them. Dani opened her eyes to find him watching her, breathing heavily.

"You truly wanted this." His brown eyes jumped between hers. "You want to know me."

"I do." She swallowed, focusing on the corner of his mouth. "But you're not sure."

"I - I'm not." He blinked. "I mean I wasn't. I don't know."

Her shoulders dropped, her chest hitching as she breathed one word. "Why?"

He drew a deep breath and leaned his forehead against hers. He pressed her hand against his heart. "I'm broken, Dani. This body and my blood is all yours, but my heart…" His fingers tightened when she tried to pull away. "There is nothing in me that doubts what we will be together." He tipped his head to the sky with a shake. "But I have to be honest with you." His voice cracked. "I don't know how to stop loving Leis."

He hated the way the light in her face dimmed, replaced by the piercing determination that made her the stunt rider, the dancer, the hacker she was. Her chin ticked up as she swallowed back the pain he knew he'd caused her.

"Dani." Her name fell out of him as a plea. "Give me time." Her throat bobbed and he stroked her cheek. "I will never intentionally hurt you, but we can't do this," he swiped a thumb across her lip to remove a spot of his blood, "we can't be this connected without being completely honest. I've spent the last few years lying to everyone, including myself. I don't want do that with you."

She looked to the sky then back to his face. Her eyes were shattered when they met his again. "What happened to you and Leis was not your fault, but how you move forward - how *we* move forward - is up to you to decide." Her eyes searched his. "I'm here with you. But you have to promise to let me in."

He held her gaze, letting her see the turmoil inside him and fighting the urge not to. "I've never let anyone close." He gestured up the path. "The dancing, the bike. No one knows about any of it."

"Why?" She folded their hands together. "Talk to me."

He ran his thumb over her knuckles, wondering at how natural it felt to hold her hand. "I wanted to see how long I could keep something from my grandmother." He leaned back against the tree. "I signed up for dance classes to see if she would notice the change in my schedule. She didn't. I kept it up using a false name. Andrew covered for me sometimes, but she never suspected anything." He tucked his opposite hand into his pocket, feeling for the bike key. "I bought a motorcycle and kept it in a storage unit on the other side of town. I kept it from everyone."

"You learned how to hide," she said softly.

"I got really good at it." He rested his head back. "Not even Leis knew. I wanted to tell her, but I was afraid she'd want to go ride with me or go to one of the dance lessons. But by then, I was enjoying having something no one else knew about."

"That sounds really lonely."

He huffed. "It was." He pulled her closer, wrapping their joined hands behind her back. He couldn't hold back the contented sigh when she placed her free palm on his chest. "You have no idea how isolated I was. Leis was the only one I trusted, and I couldn't even tell her." He covered her hand with his. "When I found out the truth, I didn't let myself think about what would happen to me. I just knew I had to get her out."

"You're both out," she said firmly. "She would want you to be happy, wouldn't she?"

He closed his eyes. "She would. She does."

She pressed her forehead to his chest, inhaling with a shudder. "Thank you for being honest with me." She looked up, straightening enough to put space between them. "I won't pretend to understand, and I will probably be a hothead about it sometimes, but if we promise to be honest about our feelings, we can work it out."

"Together." He brushed the hair out of her eyes, leaning down for a lingering kiss.

"Together." She nodded firmly and gripped his forearms. "We'll figure this out together." Her slow exhale loosened the tension in both of them, and he blinked as she took deep breaths. He copied her, lowering both their heart rates and slowing their breaths.

"See?" Her smile almost felt genuine. "If we focus on learning how our gifts work together, it will be fine." She gave his arm a squeeze and made to step away from him. "We should get back."

He held her still, searching her face. "Thank you."

"I only know part of what you've been through." The smoky tang of her anger swelled again. "Your grandmother is responsible. We will take her down, and we will re-unite the Vampir." Her eyes hardened. "And then we'll make her pay for what she's done to all of you."

He pulled her tight to his chest, tucking her under his chin. "Together. We absolutely will."

The End
...but turn the page for bonus content.

BONUS CONTENT

I've never done character interviews before writing a novel.

Most of the time the characters are strong personalities that come alive as I write. But Baden was different. His story is one the readers of the series have been asking for, but he's silent as a wraith. As I tried to write, his reactions and responses in the story were inconsistent and it became harder and harder to force the story forward with no idea what he was thinking, feeling, or wanting.

So, I decided to do an interview. Like an ACTUAL interview with him as if I'm sitting across a table with him asking him questions. 600 words into it, I realized something I always suspected about him.

He hates the spotlight and would much rather his story not be told. He's damaged, hurting, and lost. None of which he wants anyone to know, least of all a bunch of strangers who will read his novella. I truly think he would have preferred to suffer in silence than get his happily-ever-after.

Thankfully, neither me nor his mate, Dani, would allow that!

Enjoy.

I am having trouble figuring you out, Baden. Help me understand how you're feeling and what you want right now.

I just had every relationship stripped from me, I got shipped out of the country to get me out of the way because I've become a liability, and you want to know how I feel?

Okay, that's totally fair. Let's start with something simpler.

Why does this matter?

I need to know what you are looking for. What do believe about yourself?

That I am much better off not doing interviews or having my deepest darkest secrets laid out for the world to read.

*That's a bit dramatic. *considers* Though, as the author, it would be amazing if the whole world read your story.*

And you wonder why I don't want to talk to you.

Sorry. I can make sure your desire for privacy comes out in your story. But, you do know others want to know what happened to you?

Sigh Yes.

Then help me tell your story. What you believe about yourself. What do you want most?

For Leis to be safe.

That's a given. Don't think about it too much. You've just met Dani. What happened?

Honestly, I'm angry.

Why?

Because it feels like I've been set up.

By who?

Well, you are the author.

True, but I'm here asking you because I'm stuck. I'm asking for YOU to tell your side of the story. Who set you up?

Ellen and Jordan.

How?

Jordan let me believe she was a male.

She didn't know if she could trust you, and besides, no hacker uses their true name. Well, it is her true name, but you know what I mean. You use Allen. Sounds like an old man.

He rolls his eyes. Again, you gave me that name.

How did Ellen set you up?

She knew Dani and I were mates but didn't tell me.

She didn't tell you because she knew you would react the way you are now. If she'd told you, you wouldn't have gone to the studio in Dublin.

No, I wouldn't have.

You would have disappeared and never found your mate. You wouldn't have met Dani. Do you not want to have a mate?

I don't deserve her.

Yes, you do. Tell me why you think that?

I won't be able to love her the way she needs me to.

And what do you think that looks like?

Affection. Compliments. Flowers.

What if that's not what she wants?

Every female wants that.

Would it surprise you to learn she doesn't?

So, you know her, but not me.

She's not been hurt like you have. She didn't have to shut everyone out to keep them safe, so yes. I do know her a little better. Would you like to know what she wants in a mate?

side eye You're going to tell me anyway, aren't you?

I think you need to know...Long motorcycle rides through the country. Working out and studio time to practice for your performances. You doing what you say you'll do. Helping her take care of the house and cleaning up after yourself.

That's not so hard to do.

So...if she wanted to support you, what would be the best way for her to do that?

silence

Look. I know you've kept to yourself for years. You were always the strong one, the one everyone counted on, but never acknowledged. That sucks, and I'm sorry your story has led you here. But I want more than anything to give you a happy ending. I've always planned it that way, and Dani is waiting for you.

She's gorgeous, so thank you for that at least.

There's more to her than that, and you know it.

leans forward to rest his elbows on his knees She's wicked smart, funny, loyal, and loves her family more than anyone I know.

Except you.

Except me. The one who lost his entire family.

No. You didn't. You just had to go away for a couple weeks for their safety and yours. And Dani's family will be yours. It's huge. You'll never be alone again.

That's…That sounds amazing.

I smile See? Telling me what you want wasn't so hard, was it?

What I want and what I get are two different things.

Not in this case they aren't. Tell me what else you want.

I lay a hand on his arm, but he pulls away

I hold up my hands

Right. No affection.

Explain why I can't ease into the relationship with Dani? Why does it have to happen so fast?

Because you need to let someone in before you implode. You can't keep locking all these feelings away, they are eating you alive. She scented it the first time you met.

And feels sorry for me.

No, she doesn't. She knows your history, the facts of it at least. She gets why you're angry and closed off. You can trust her with your feelings.

scoffs Feelings. All I feel is anger.

That's actually hurt and fear.

What, are you a psychiatrist now?

No, but I know the root of anger is usually fear due to not having control, add to that the betrayal of your grandmother and Leis's mom… what you're feeling is justified. But Dani can help you heal.

How?

By giving you a safe place to be the real you.

She'll run if she ever sees the real me.

She'll run if she doesn't. She can take your worst, but she can't take your silence. I built her strong minded, emotionally intelligent, and I surrounded her with the kind of powerful support system you never had. Tap into her resources. I created her just for you.

he swallows repeatedly, his jaw sawing This is terrifying.

What is?

Emotions. They hurt.

Yeah, they do but keeping them locked up will destroy you. It almost has.

Let me sleep on it. I'll try to do better tomorrow.

Thank you.

Reaches to pat his arm

glares

scratches back of my head

Right. I'll meet you back here tomorrow morning.

About the Author

Michelle Bolanger is a Christian author of contemporary and speculative fiction. She also writes non-fiction articles that share the hope of Christ through daily life lessons as a wife, author, and child of God. In addition to her writing, she is also a talented vocalist and enjoys painting. She lives in small town Ohio with her husband. Together, they enjoy going on long cruises, motorcycle rides along side roads and back roads, and cheering for their favorite professional hockey teams.

After 30+ years of mid-level management in banking and finance, Michelle left the corporate life to pursue her creative passions. She has co-lead Biblical courses on personal finance and budgeting, and served as the women's ministry co-ordinator for her local church where she crafted Bible studies and taught women how to apply Biblical principles to their daily lives. As a vocalist, she has served as a member of her church's worship team, leading the congregation into a deeper connection with God through song.

She began her publishing journey in 2015 with her urban fantasy debut novel, *"The Kiss"* the first book in a young adult series now titled *"The Divided Hearts Series."* She also published the first two stand alone contemporary novels in a collection of gritty, hot button stories that follow characters who come to faith in Christ after walking through some topics most Christian novelists won't write about. She tackles topics like LGBTQ, human trafficking, abortion, and adultery.

Michelle and her husband host a small group Bible study in their home once a week, and she has plans to expand her teaching and encouraging opportunities in the future by organizing an in person writer's group for writers of all levels in her local area. Her greatest desire is to demonstrate the hope of faith in Christ by sharing the lessons God is teaching her as she continues to publish new stories, grow her business, and encourage other writers and women in their giftings and callings.

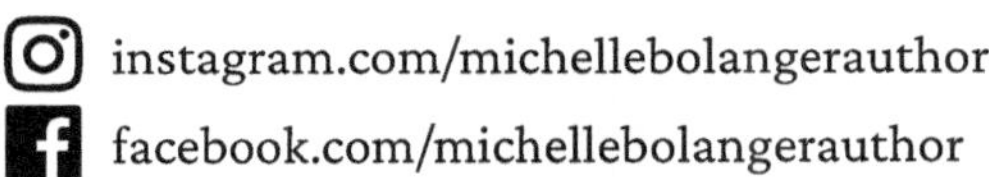

instagram.com/michellebolangerauthor
facebook.com/michellebolangerauthor

Connect with Michelle

Find me online:
Website: michellebolanger.com
Socials: @michellebolangerauthor
Email: Michelle@risenfiction.com

www.ingramcontent.com/pod-product-compliance
Lightning Source LLC
Chambersburg PA
CBHW040910010826
48978CB00013BB/1234